BANNISTER
DOLL

SYLVIA DAVEY

This is a work of fiction, based on some of my youthful memories. A friend and I did spend some of one school summer holiday in our local cemetery, but the characters and events described herein are imaginary, although there may be references to specific places and people as I remember them.

ONE

That first time we saw him, he was leaning against the old tombstone, the tombstone which only that week, we had claimed as ours. He was sitting on the ground where we had, just the day before, finished clearing the overgrown mass of weeds and couch grass which had covered the burial area. I will always carry that face within me somewhere, a face so pale and tired, as if all the energy of him had drained away. We said that he looked lifeless. We hardly knew then how accurate that description would turn out to be. He told us his name was Jack and that he had climbed over the cemetery wall behind the grave. He didn't exactly tell us that. He didn't speak in sentences. But he did answer some of our questions. Mostly one word answers to the most basic of questions. And only when he felt like it. We had to be patient. Totally surprised by his unexpected appearance and not knowing what to make of him, we guessed that, like us, he'd wanted to sit in the sun on the bed of the grave mound. It was a glorious day at the start of the summer holidays. That wall he said he'd climbed over was an old stone one, much higher than we could see over and we couldn't work out how he could have had the strength to get himself up and over such a height. There didn't seem to be any toe holes for him to climb up, or cracks where he would have been able to grip with his fingers. It was too high, we thought, for him to have leapt down from the top, even supposing the wall's other side was easier to climb. We both had a go at it, climbing our side ourselves, as he made no effort to look in our direction when we went behind the tombstone. There was no-one to see us show ourselves up. I considered myself a bit of a tomboy at times in those days and I couldn't do it. My friend Linda had no chance. Nor could we understand why he should want to sit on a grave. There were plenty of seats scattered here and there around the cemetery.

Sitting on graves wasn't a young lad's pastime; it wasn't anyone's pastime as far as I could see. We were pretty weird being there ourselves, two teenage girls spending their school summer holiday in a cemetery. Who would want to join us? I couldn't understand the boy's words either. His voice had a soft rasping quality to it. It was as if he had pebbles in his mouth and he was struggling to speak through them. We strained forward to listen to what he was saying. He was a skinny thing too. You could almost see the outline of every bone through his shirt. My grandmother would have said he needed fattening up. When Linda said later that he looked like a ghost, I understood exactly what she meant. He was exactly like what we would have expected a ghost to be … pale, wan, spectral. I laughed even though looking at him was certainly unsettling. I laughed because I didn't believe in ghosts. But he made me nervous. Linda's words made me nervous. Actually, they made me more than nervous. I felt a chill running down my back and laughed to make it go away. I just tried to ignore what she'd said. It wasn't possible in spite of what I felt. I just didn't believe in ghosts.

The boy was in a lovely place to sunbathe, if that was what he was doing and it was a glorious day for it. Maybe the sun on his face would put some life, some colour, back into him? The sun had drawn Linda and me out to enjoy the day too and he had chosen the very spot we had chosen for ourselves on previous visits to the cemetery. We had walked all around this old section of the cemetery before choosing it. It was the best spot in the place in our opinion. It was away from the other cemetery alley ways in a quiet and secluded location. A couple of old, thickly leaved and thickly trunked trees hid the grave from the main cemetery thoroughfare. It was a private and out of sight place, ideal for two teenage girls to carry on their secret gossiping. Now, you might think that a cemetery was not really the sort of place two young girls would want to spend any time, even if their conversations were entirely personal and intimate. Actually, our talk was scarcely confidential at all. We were innocents in the world at that stage, sweet fourteen and never been kissed. But we were certainly interested in the opposite sex, at least in some of them, the good looking ones. Boys were an unknown world to us as we both went to single sex schools. Linda had the advantage as she had to travel miles every day to school in Lytham where she went to a private girls' school and the bus was shared daily by the boys going to Lytham's equivalent school for boys. I imagined a joyful party atmosphere every day upstairs on those buses, everyone laughing and flirting as they came and went together. It ought to have been a riotous time but Linda never said anything about it and so maybe it wasn't. Maybe they all sat dutifully with their same sex friends each day and I had nothing to be jealous about. Maybe single sex schools presented some sort of barrier to intermingling. I eventually went out with a boy from the Lytham Boys' School. He must have shared the bus each day with Linda and the other girls but he never spoke of her and she never mentioned him, though she knew much later on that he was my boyfriend.

9

Anyway, throughout those summer days Linda and I mostly gossiped with a few rude and critical words about the girls we considered our rivals at the Ribbleton Youth Club, but there were no state secrets or critical revelations. We knew nothing about anything in those days. The wisdom of modern youth astonishes me now. But that's another story. I'm not really sure how we came to be there that day or how we came to be spending so much of our time in the cemetery during that summer in the first place. Why hadn't we just chosen one our bedrooms or a back garden? The only explanation I can come up with was perhaps that gardens and bedrooms were in the vicinity of parents, mothers, and even more particularly, younger brothers and sisters? Younger siblings were the bane of our lives as we stabbed naively at the beginnings of adulthood. Or maybe it was because the cemetery represented freedom? No-one ever knew or even asked where we were going or where we'd been. Grown-ups didn't in those days. You could disappear for the whole day; the adults only began to worry if you didn't turn up home at teatime. They rarely provided us with entertainment. We had to make our own. 'Teatime', that's a giveaway too, isn't it? We were northerners, but we were never aware of that either. We didn't think much about the world beyond our small part of it. We knew it existed but it mostly lay somewhere beyond our horizons. The cemetery, on the contrary, wasn't too far from where both of us lived and it was free, unlike the Pinewood Coffee Club in Preston, where many of our peers seemed to be spending their summer holidays that year. We imagined them sitting in an overcrowded room, in a fog of sweaty bodies and smoke, flaunting the illicit cigarettes which most of them weren't legally old enough to smoke. They would be paying for one coffee after another and believing that their flirting with the boys from the Grammar School or wherever, would lead to something more exciting. Admittedly boys were no attraction in our graveyard setting but they would be having conversations similar to ours, only shared

11

with every listening ear, whereas we had chosen the fresh air, the wildness of the neglected graves and the company of the occasional old codger grave-diggers. We didn't invite any of the others to come and join us. They probably wouldn't have come anyway. They would perhaps have thought we were slightly mad and would have jeered at us and revelled in passing on the information of our holiday high jinks to everyone else for further ridicule. We were weird, as I've already said. And, we didn't care. We never heard any of that and so it didn't bother us. We were happy in our secluded weirdness.

I cannot remember whose idea it was to explore the cemetery in the first place. It may have been mine as I still like investigating cemeteries, especially the really old ones, the ones battered by time, weathered in weeds and full of long dead and sadly forgotten people. The best and most evocative graveyard I've ever seen was in Dallas, Texas, of all places, slap bang in the middle of all the noise and traffic of a sky-high American city based on oil and greed. The sparse and ancient tombstones there sloped and slanted in all directions, with, not far away, a wonderful herd of bronze cattle to keep them company. The guide book said there were forty-nine of them, all larger than life and slippery enough to discourage any would-be modern teenage cowboys from mounting. Some equally bronze and lifeless cowherds, three of them, looked out over the herd astride bronze horses, as the cows meandered downhill through a running creek. They were supposedly being driven to market, and were intended to commemorate the old days before Dallas discovered oil. They were all magnificent.

I also admired the few abandoned graves on the cliffs near Reculver in Kent, where I was later to live. It was just beyond Herne Bay. Most of the nearby houses of the original village had eroded into the sea and probably taken the other graves with them. There are just these few left … three I think … to mark the history of the place, with inscriptions that are largely illegible. The church itself still had its old towers and some of its walls, that was all, but it was a remarkable landmark for the edge of the bay. It had the added interest of a Roman fort next door, lost to the centuries but with signs telling what would have been there if you looked where they indicated. There was a bit of Roman wall. Reculver is a spot that has been inhabited over hundreds of years.

The part of Ribbleton cemetery we had chosen was exactly like those cemeteries, but more extensive, the graves old, forgotten and weathered by time. Linda's father was the local vicar and so perhaps she had some sort of affinity with cemeteries and maybe she'd been the one to drag us both there? Vicars must spend a fair amount of their working lives in such places after all. Such a conclusion would, however, have considerably annoyed my friend.

'It's not as if I have the word Bible imprinted across my forehead,' she would say when she felt someone was thinking that a vicar's daughter ought to be prim and proper, which she most certainly was not. She was fair and square and straight to the point. She said what she thought and she thought what she said. She blamed this supposed coyness, most definitely an unwanted role, as the explanation for most of the Youth Club boys seem-ing uncomfortable in her company. Her father was the vicar of the church we all attended and a serious and forbidding man at that. They all knew it. Maybe the idea of him looming over them with frowns was slightly off putting? The church thing was not be-cause any of us was brimming over with religion; it was just what one did in those days; go to church on Sundays and meet with friends from there on Wednesdays and Sunday evenings at the Youth Club. Sometimes there was a Saturday Night Dance organised by that same Youth Club. It was the main focus of our social life, of every young person's life at that time. All my school friends had similar churches to go to in their areas and we used to go to each other's Saturday night dances. The Catholics were perhaps an exception. They didn't seem to have a Youth Club. They might have done. It's just that I never heard of one. That was the way of things when I was growing up. We didn't really mix once we'd left junior school or even before that. Each religion had its own schools. The only cross over was when parents paid for a private school and my parents had certainly never done that. The Catholics didn't seem to have dances either and came to ours instead, if they were allowed. By their parents, I mean. We had no objections. We felt sorry for them. I don't remember going to a Catholic Youth Club dance at all.

Preston Cemetery seemed to me then to be an enormous and impressive place. It lay off the main road through Ribbleton. There were huge gates leading into it and I felt that such grandeur suggested that the avenue, which opened up from them, could only lead to some imposing stately home. The graves were far beyond the gates and out of sight. The wide avenue led the visitor to them, an avenue bordered with broad stretches of carefully manicured lawns with 'Keep off the Grass' signs at regular intervals. The supreme wickedness then for me was setting a foot on the greenness just to prove I could.

When my cousin came to stay from Llandudno, she saw the beckoning gates when we went to buy ice creams at Cuff's where the ice cream was home-made and, according to locals, the best in the world. I still believe that! It was delicious. Does the shop even exist now? I can still feel my ancient pride in Cuff's and those magnificent cemetery gates. She didn't believe me when I told her what the place really was. We had to walk to the end of the first avenue and see the graves stretching away ahead of us before she would accept otherwise. This gave us a view of the modern section of the cemetery, a huge expanse of marble and granite headstones with white or green chippings shining in the sunshine. We could have got lost in those repetitive pathways with their equally repetitive rectangular graves, except that you could see right across the open space in front of you, a vista of flatness, broken occasionally by a mound around a hole being prepared for a new occupant or a heaping up of funeral bouquets left abandoned by the latest deceased's nearest and dearest. This section of the cemetery seemed a sad and dismal place to us. Boringly modern, flat and all the same. New graves were colourful at first with their flowers and wreaths and Linda and I fell upon them at once to read with ghoulish delight the messages left behind. They were worded as if the dear departed was going to rise up and read them once those tearful mourners had returned home. We were too young to appreciate the grieving loss and despair they represented but we did understand the sadness later when those flowers were shrivelled and rotting only a week afterwards in their rain spattered cellophane. And then later again, when we came upon those same bouquets consigned to one of the cemetery bins which stood like sentinels on each path corner. There was usually a dripping tap next to them. The bins overflowed with dead or dying flowers, waiting for the gravediggers to take them away. Then the weeds arrived on the grave mounds as the earth sank down, taking all those memories into the depths with them. Sometimes the graves were subsequently cared for and sometimes not. Sometimes, headstones were installed and sometimes the graves were left to the elements and forgotten. We learned early the hypocrisy of false endearments.

The new section was where we eventually made contact with the gravediggers. There were three of them. They were there digging or filling in, placing or removing the flowers, and they must have seen us as we circulated around the place. But at first we kept our distance. We never went anywhere near where they were working because we had an 'idee fixte' in our heads that they were old and dirtied by the work they did and in consequence were the 'dirty old men' we had always been warned about. We had only a hazy idea about what the expression meant but their dirty overalls classified them and we knew that we were supposed to steer clear of them because such men were dangerous in some inexplicable way. We did suspect that it was something to do with sex but quite how, we did not understand. As I've said, we were innocents and nothing like the teenagers of modern times who know far more than is good for them. These 'unsavoury' gravediggers waved at us and shouted 'hello' but we just stuck our noses in the air as if they were bad smells and carried on through the cemetery towards the out of sight old section. We did notice that one of the three seemed a lot younger than his mates but as he was just as dirty as they were, his dirtiness lumped him into the same category.

The old section of the cemetery seemed prehistoric to us, though it probably wasn't as old as we believed. Preston had played its part in history and we both knew its name had come from a forgotten time when it had been a 'priests' town', a place with a sizeable monastery or other kind of religious foundation. There had also been a famous battle near where we both lived, something to do with Oliver Cromwell and King Charles 1. I lived in Langdale Road and knew that Langdale had been a leader in the English Civil War, a battle I'd vaguely heard of as being between the Royalist supporters of the King and the Roundheads led by Oliver Cromwell. I had heard some story that the Roundheads had pudding bowl haircuts and hence the name. I had no idea which side Langdale was on, but someone told me he had been called Marmaduke, which was funny enough. Other roads were named after more characters from the period. There was a Cromwell Road, a Hamilton Road, a Fairfax Road, a Lambert Road and even a royal Stuart Road, which led up to where Linda lived.

Quite reasonably, all this caused us to believe in the antique origins of the cemetery but in retrospect it probably only went as far back as the industrial foundation of the town, when the town's population expanded at the time of the Industrial Revolution as people came to work in the ever increasing number of cotton mills. As a result, there would have been lots more people to be buried, which explained the need for a big cemetery like Ribbleton's. It probably only dated back to the early nineteenth century but the old section seemed ancient to us in comparison to the new one. Here the headstones were old stone, blackened by time, hidden in moss and in some cases leaning aslant as if the elements were slowly returning them to the earth. The dates impressed us and took us back to a time when people died young and babies and children had scarcely any life at all.

The horror of it all fascinated us. There were huge family lists with daughters and sons of the above who had not even managed to reach double figures. Linda and I vied with one another to find the youngest dead child or the most pitiable married couple who had outlived the greatest number of children. We competed to find the oldest date and the oldest occupant and selected out all the weird names for each other to laugh at. There were lots of Samuels, Isiahs and Nathaniels and for the females there seemed to be countless attempts to instil in the girls such praiseworthy virtues as Charity, Mercy and Humility. Marmaduke Langdale would have fitted in very well here, if perhaps a bit 'posh'. Again, we were not totally heartless but the dates seemed so far away from our lives that we struggled to understand that we ought not to be disrespectful or find some treasured child's name a source of amusement. We were disgracefully lacking in sympathy. But we were enthralled by the idea of the forgotten world we had found.

 There was an overwhelming sense of neglect everywhere we looked. There was not a grave that was cared for. There were trees and bushes but they had all outgrown their planting positions. All these resting places must have once been well tended. All these relatives must have come to visit in their Victorian, Edwardian or Georgian clothes, and they must have cleared weeds, trimmed the grass between the graves and planted flowers for their dear departed. Now every plot had been reclaimed by heartless nature. We trekked through knee-high weeds to read the inscriptions, scratched our arms on overgrown and unpruned rose bushes, scraped away at moss to read whatever was hidden. And no-one came near. It must have been an eerie place at night. We happily shuddered at the idea of walking through here in the dark, an owl hooting above us, the spiders out on their webs. We would have jumped at the slightest twitch of grass nearby. But in reality, we would never have been there to hear them!

But time had passed and all those faithful and tending visitors of the past were all now dead themselves. There was no-one left to come. We were traipsing through a secret domain. The trees and overgrown shrubs hid us from the world and it was clear from the height and quantity of the weeds that the world wasn't interested in finding us anyway.

'We could have a secret den here,' said Linda, forgetting that we were now supposed to be older and should have put away our childish ideas. Dens were for silly younger brothers. Linda and I both had one of those. Linda had a younger sister as well.

'Yeah, that would be great' I agreed, also forgetting that I too liked to consider myself a bit grown up now. We both knew we weren't going to play at being members of any Black Hand Gang. We were just thinking of somewhere quiet, a private place to sit. And we soon found the ideal place at that old stone tombstone.

The grave was right at the edge of the old cemetery, hidden behind tall overgrown bushes on the graves directly in front of it. Behind was the old cemetery wall, so high that we couldn't be overlooked on that side either. And there were old trees. I mean really old trees. There would be shade on hot days. We were hopeful we might have a few of those. And if the weather ever turned whilst we were in situ, there was a thick canopy of leaves to offer some protection from any rain. The headstone was suitably interesting with several entries and a mixture of old and young names and ages. The whole place felt like it had drawn us towards it. How could we have found it behind those bushes if the grave had not been waiting to be found? Why would we have agreed on it so instantly if it had not been meant to be? There was no arguing about sites. It was as if this spot was intended to be ours. We both somehow knew it. Linda threw herself down on the coarse grass on the mound and shaded her eyes as she turned her head in every direction.

'When I die you can put me in here. It's such a restful place. There is peace on every side.'

'When you are dead, there will be just four wood-end walls on every side. The inside of your coffin. It may well be peaceful but will you like it as much then?

She sat up immediately. 'Yes, well. That will be a long time in the future.'

'Do you even want to be buried?' I asked, sitting down beside her. There was just room for the two of us. I thought of lovers entwined in death benea*th us.* There would have been enough room for two bodies but not if they were in separate coffins. 'Or would you prefer to be cremated?'

'I don't know. I've never thought about it. What about you?'

I had not even been to a funeral at that stage in my life; my first would be my grandfather's when I was at university. I had never seen a coffin, had certainly never seen a dead body. My first body was years later, an eleven year old girl, a pupil, who had died of an infection after a bone marrow transplant. She had been a lovely, shy girl who had always smiled timidly through her suffering. The family had invited the school staff to visit to pay their respects the day she had been brought home from the hospital. She hadn't been smiling then, I remembered, as she lay there in her coffin with cotton wool stuck up her nostrils. It's the cotton wool which haunts me. I would have preferred to have been able to remember her in her timid and bashful mode. I have never chosen to visit a dead person at the mortuary since.

I had thought about death though and liking history, had searched out all the ghoulish things which whet children's appetites, girls as much as boys. I was interested in the Plague of London, with its 'bring out your dead' carts and mass graves spread with quick lime. I enjoyed all the gory details about symptoms and the rapidity of how the boils had developed. I had thought about the people who went round painting crosses in red paint on the doors of ill-fated houses. Then there was Queen Anne with her 18 dead children. How had she coped with that? I visualised 18 little coffins. I knew about Burke and Hare murdering to obtain bodies for anatomical dissections up in Scotland and the cursed grave robbers from the pyramids of Egypt, thieves wanting all the luxurious paraphernalia which accompanied a dead Pharaoh into the Afterlife. I selected a suitably grisly piece of my knowledge for Linda.

'Did you know that little bells were often put in coffins along with the dead body in case the person wasn't really dead and needed to be rescued? They were supposed to ring the bell to attract attention.'

'But what if there was nobody there to hear?'

Linda's face was earnest and worried together.

'What if everyone had gone home after the funeral?'

I shrugged.

'Tough luck. Somebody even invented a coffin that had a string you could pull from inside which would ring a bell above the grave.'

'That sounds better. But imagine if you were sitting there at the funeral when the bell began ringing.'

I felt the hairs on the back of my neck rise. I shuddered. But that didn't stop me.

'And did you know that George Washington told his servants that he hadn't to be buried for several days to give him a chance to come back to life if he wasn't really dead?

Linda's face was contorting beyond reality. She was dramatising her disgust. But she overdid it. We

29

both ended up laughing. She stood up in apparent rage. 'I don't think we should come here in the first place if all you're going to do is scare me with cemetery tales.'

I grinned and tugged her back down. 'Sorry, but I think you're enjoying the stories. I don't believe you're scared at all.'

Linda made a ghoulish face to intimidate me and sat down again.' I think we should each bring a spooky story every time we come here to read to each other. It could be a ghost story or just a scary tale. What do you think?'

'That sounds like too much hard work to me. Where are we going to find all these stories? Seems like homework. No thanks. It's the holidays. 'Actually, I think a rug might be better if we're going to bring anything. To sit on. This long grass is really getting on my nerves. It scratches. I'm itching all over. I'm sure there are creepy crawlies getting at me. Good job I don't suffer from hay fever either. Do you?'

'No, thank goodness. If we're having a rug, perhaps we could have a book to read? Or maybe an apple or some sweets?

'I don't want to be reading. I can do that at home.'

'Okay, but we could have things to eat, couldn't we?' I suppose so. And to start with, if you want to read, why don't we read the gravestone here? We ought to know who we're sitting on. Or next to. Don't you think?'

We settled ourselves on the mound in front of the headstone and went down the names. I've had to think hard to remember some of those names now, after all the intervening years. Certainly, the dates have gone from my brain forever. We didn't think about dates much then, too much like having to re-vise for history at school. I'd had enough of them.

I think the dates here were all early 1800s and per-haps amongst the earliest graves in the cemetery. Our chosen spot might have been where the first graves were set out.

The list was headed by a woman. Was she Sarah or

Sandra? It was hard to read the grime covered stonework. Or perhaps it was something complete ly different? We thought ourselves very clever when we deduced that she must have died in child-birth. Her death was so close to the death of the girl named below hers, her daughter, we guessed. The child was not even a month old. The poor babe must have struggled on for a while after Sarah, Sandra or whatever, and then just passed. The death of another child in the family followed a few years later, this time a son, who died at the age of eleven. After the death of his mother the boy must have been brought up by his father who was at the bottom of the family list of names. The father was John and he had out-lived all the rest of his family. He had been seven-tyish when he died, according to his dates, which we reckoned to be a good age when we compared that relative longevity with the ages of the so-called el-derly fathers and mothers resting in peace in the nearby graves. I particularly remember that. He had outlived a second son, also named John, who died aged fifteen. We imagined Father John trying to keep his family together without the help of his wife beside him. We pictured him having to earn a wage somewhere in one of Preston's many cotton mills, toiling long hours for a penance which wasn't nearly enough to feed and clothe his two growing lads. First one son died, then another. And, we were already forgetting, the baby we had found first.

We weren't particularly shocked. It was a tale we had come across many times in the old cemetery. It was Victorian England. We knew all about it. Our history teachers had so effectively filled our young imaginations with all the horrors of the Industrial Revolution that we quite overlooked the fact that anyone who could afford a sizeable head stone like the one we were reading, as well as hire an engraver to record the family names on it, was not as poor and long suffering as we imagined. We may have been right to shed our pity for him as a widower and a man who had lost three of his children but he was a relatively lucky man when set beside his fellow

33

citizens. He had lived a long and fruitful life.

The engraved names didn't tell us how any of them had died and we didn't worry too much about them. We were just glad to be alive ourselves and even more relieved that we hadn't had the misfortune to be born when death and disease had been so commonplace. I am surprised I can remember as much as I have, as we had very little to say about the family. We were more concerned with what we were going to wear at the Youth Club Dance coming up the weekend after next. Linda was working on her mother, trying to get her to buy her a new pair of shoes. She knew exactly the pair she wanted having seen them in a shoe shop window in the town centre in transit from the bus coming home from Lytham, and catching the Ribbleton bus. I wasn't too impressed when she described them. Even she called them granny shoes, the sort she said old ladies wore. They had high chunky heels and tied up with ribbons down the front. She must have recognised the doubts on my face as she immediately said it was me who was old fashioned. These shoes would be the latest thing and I, who went out mincing around in little high heeled brown crocodile skin patterned court shoes, was totally out of date.

I had a big clunky brown bag, also in crocodile skin, which exactly matched my crocodile shoes and I thought I was co-ordinated elegance. Looking back, my shoes and bag were all most definitely simulated plastic, but I was happy in my ignorance then, and now, with the importance of protecting the environment, even pleased.

My mother had also got me some gloves to wear with my outfit, though even I acknowledged that these were beyond dated. They were not keeping you warm in winter gloves. They were spotlessly white, summer gloves to be worn by well brought up young ladies. I may have been a well brought up young lady and I may initially have gone out wearing them, but they were stuffed tightly into my coat pocket as soon as I was round the corner; and then I put them back on again on the bus as I went home.

TWO

Linda got her shoes. She wore them the week after at the Wednesday Youth Club session.

'What do you think?' she asked, doing a little parade around the side room before the table tennis had got underway

'Okay,' I said, with as many smiles as I could get onto my face. Actually, they were not as fearsome as I had anticipated. I may even have been won over to wearing them myself, perhaps for school or if I ever be-came a nurse. In plain black leather with black ribbons, she was able to play table tennis quite com-fortably in them. That tells you what they were like. Even then, they were probably better than the shoes I got to wear for school, stately Miss Prim lace ups my mother bought for me, which she claimed would give me lots of support around my ankles. I called them clod hoppers and watched enviously as the shoes of my school fellows got daintier and more slim-line day by day. I consoled myself now with the thought that Linda's shoes would not be impressing anyone at the Youth Club Dance being planned for that Saturday. At least I was allowed to wear my crocodile shoes for going out in. But then Linda was probably not into impressing anyone. She liked to go her own way. I think she was moving into some sort of hippy stage with a vision of life as free and easy, and with flowers in her hair. She was currently drooling over Donovan, whom I had barely heard of at that point. When I saw him later on 'Top of the Pops', I had to agree that he was what we then called 'rather dishy'. Not much older than us either and his song 'Catch the Wind' was also pretty good. I could see where Linda was coming from but there was no-one like Donovan at the Youth Club and no-one likely to turn up looking like him on Saturday night either.

Linda was trying to settle for Dave Appleton as the next best available lookalike in the neighbourhood, but since there were too many other local girls chasing him already, it didn't seem like she was destined for success. I was toddling along behind with my eye on Frank Ridden. Frank and I had gone to the same primary school, Greenlands, and he had liked me there, but the eleven plus had divided our ways and he had gone forward to supposedly better things at the local Sec Mod. He was currently chasing a dull looking girl called Lindsey. So was Dave Appleton, and the outlook looked equally bleak for me too. Linda and I had a lot to say on occasions about Lindsey as we sat on our cemetery mound that summer. Like, what had she got that made her so attractive? We couldn't come up with any answers. We knew the obvious one, but she didn't look the sort. She was actually quite nice when we spoke to her. We couldn't understand it.

Linda was talking about wearing a hat like Donovan's too for the dance, a peaked cap rather like a French kepi, but she had to get one first. Having just got her shoes, she had doubts that she would manage it. I didn't hold out much hope for her either. The hat would be harmless but as soon as her father got a whiff of sixties style notions of free love and matched them up to the hippy look his daughter was bent on cultivating, she would be closed down. He was the vicar and seemed to me to have pretty strict ideas about his religion. I'd probably call him intolerant now, but didn't know the word then. Youth Club Sunday church attendance was fine if we all went to his church, but sometimes there were calls for us to attend inter denominational church events and Linda was never allowed to go to one of those, not even the Methodist assemblies, which surprised me. With a relapsed Methodist father myself, I couldn't see too many differences between their belief and the Church of England. But what did I know? My grandfather was actually Presbyterian but he couldn't find one of their churches when he moved from Scotland to Chorley and the Methodists were the next best thing.

I didn't think much about beliefs then. Linda wasn't allowed to go to any dances other than the ones at her father's church. I went off to the Top Rank Ballroom under Sixteens Dance Club in town with school friends most Tuesday nights. There was no alcohol and it finished, as I remember, at 10.30pm. All very sedate with plenty of time to catch the last bus home. Linda's reverend father probably kept a close watch on proceedings at our Youth club. He didn't pop in personally but his curate always did. I can remember the curate standing to the side of the stage in the church hall in his long black ecclesiastical gown. I don't think his presence ever bothered anyone. We all knew him quite well as he directed the Youth Club Christmas shows. I was in Robin Hood one year but only as one of the drippy dancers who came on to mask scene changing. We sang dreary out of date show songs like 'The Sun Has Got his Hat On' and had lurid over-made up faces. At least the others did. The amateur make-up artist, someone's Mum, said my face was greasy enough already and hardly put anything on me. My Mum consoled me, saying a greasy skin would be a bonus in later life, preserving me from wrinkles! I'm still not convinced! Actually, my

Mum always said 'oily'. 'Greasy' was one of her distasteful words. She had a lot of those. I mainly remember 'lousy' and 'bum'. I was not allowed to say those under pain of being ignored for a very long time. She said they offended her ears! Strangely, as a teacher years later, I found myself saying much the same thing myself to some pupil, telling some kid that my ears were offended. He … they were nearly always boys … probably wondered what on earth I was talking about. Except that by then, in some of the disciplinary situations I found myself dealing with, the language probably was really offensive to my ears. I and the Youth Club members, and especially my Mum, were all pretty innocent in those days.

  Whatever, the curate's presence probably reassured the vicar that his daughter would be safe and sound. As were the rest of us. Linda would have been equally safe at the Top Rank sessions. I never saw any trouble there, not a fight, not a sneaky bit of snogging or any other examples of the kind of naughtiness which the Reverend seemed to imagine was rife.

After playing table tennis, Linda and I got called into a Youth Club Committee meeting. We'd felt quite honoured when we had been invited to be on the committee. It seemed like a step forward to some sort of acclaim. After all, we had been chosen; there were no elections. We soon realised that our opinions were not being invited. Our ability to do the grotty jobs Youth Club sessions required was our main qualification for the promotion. We were being honoured with getting to do the jobs which the more established, that is older, committee members, wanted to shift off their own shoulders. They must have realised we were reliable. Linda would always turn up because it was the only chance she got to go out in mixed company and I would simply tag along. On Youth Club nights we would put out and put away the chairs around the room. We did a stint on the 'Snack Bar', otherwise known as the church hall kitchen. On dance nights, the stint on the Snack Bar was longer but we were also in charge of the 'Cloak-room' for long periods. We had to set up tables across the door entrance to a side room and take in coats in return for a raffle ticket. The partner ticket had to be pinned to said coat and hung up on one of the many hooks around the room. Then we had to hope that we could find the coat again when its owner came to claim it at the end of the evening. This was the real challenge as we soon ran out of hooks and had to resort to dumping coats in piles on trestle tables around the room. Linda and I under-stood the 'system' we were using but after we'd had time off and other people had taken over the cloak-room job, the 'system' had undergone several and various changes and then retrieving a coat presented an often insurmountable task. We regularly had to invite guests into our enclave to see if they could find their own coat under the piles of coats laid upon coats and the layers of coats under coats on over-loaded hooks. If the owner's ticket matched the ticket on the coat there was often cause for outright cheering.

On the next Youth Club Dance Night, Linda wore her grandma shoes and I my crocodile titchy heels. That particular dance evening when the first rush of cloakroom customers had reduced, I crawled under the tables blocking the door and went to get us an orangeade each. I don't remember Coca Cola or Pepsi Cola in those far off days. I remember the icy slush stuff at Top Rank and chose it recently when out with my grandchildren at the seaside. I was impressed with myself as grown-ups are supposed to have tea or coffee or, if in a bar or restaurant, beer, wine or whatever. I was disappointed with the modern version of slush, but it certainly carried memories.

The Youth Club 'Bar' was directly opposite our cloakroom and when I returned with two bottles bobbing with straws, Linda's eyes were shifting meaningfully to her left. I recognised it was a supposedly discreet message and that she couldn't speak. But when I shifted my own eyes in the direction she indicated, all I could see were the people who had been queuing behind me at the bar. Linda sighed and lifted her eyebrows as if I were the most annoying person on earth. She grabbed the bottles off me so that I could crawl back under the table to join her on the other side.

'What?' I said, as if it was her fault, which caused her even greater exasperation.

'I can't say just now. Her eyes rolled left and some kind of sound grumbled forth from between her gritted teeth. 'Losh over zer!'

I think this was meant to be 'look over there.' And then suddenly, with a final groan and much more clearly, 'oh, he's gone now.'

'So, who have I missed?'

'One of the gravediggers.'

'From the cemetery?'

'Well, that's where you usually find gravediggers.'

'Our cemetery?'

'How many other cemeteries do you know so well around here?'

45

'But which digger and what is he doing here?'

'Would you like to stop and think before you ask you ask any more daft questions? Do you really think the two old codgers would come to our Youth Club Dance here? Does that help?'

'Ah,' I said, and after another moment. 'The young one. Has he come to the dance? 'She looked at me through narrowed eyes.

'Well, unless there's been a death on the dance-floor and he's come to collect the body prior to burial, I suspect you're on the right track.'

'But he didn't bring a coat in, otherwise we'd have seen him.'

'Not everybody has one, thank goodness, otherwise the queue would have been even longer. Appeals would go out … can you imagine it? Club members lost under piles of coats.'

'Are you sure it was him?'

'Well, he didn't have his spade with him, or the other two gravediggers, the old ones, but I expect he's allowed out on his own at weekends.'

'Was he on his own then?'

'I didn't mean that literally. I didn't see who he was with. He bought two drinks and so maybe there's a glamorous blond waiting for him in the hall.'

'Did he see you?'

'Don't think so. And you had your back to him and so you wouldn't recognise him. He was in ordinary clothes. Clean and tidy. He scrubs up well.'

We were eventually relieved at our post and able to go on a break. We sidled into the church hall. It wasn't a question of tiptoeing around the place to not be seen as there was such a cacophony in there that a brass band could probably have marched among the dancers and caused little disturbance. We hid ourselves instead amongst the people standing at the back. There were an awful lot of them, mostly the lads surveying the 'ladies' and trying to determine if any of them was worth dancing with. I'm glad the social world has changed and girls no longer have to wait patiently to be chosen by some spotty youth they instantly dismiss at the end of the music. Girls rarely got a choice in those days. Gravedigger and friend were surveyors like the rest of them. We found him not far from us and so we shuffled further along the back wall. We wanted to check him out. Linda wanted to confirm that it really was him and I wanted to see what he looked like away from the cemetery. If he scrubbed as well as Linda had said, I wanted to see it for myself. There would be discussions to be had about his appearance. On no account did we want to be taken for girls chasing him. We affected a bored and nonchalant look whilst our eyes darted repeatedly in his direction and then away again. We wanted a really good look without being seen ourselves. We failed. His eyes and ours, all four of ours at once it seemed, locked with his in one sudden glance. It seemed like an age as he faltered, stared at us and then seemed to realise who we were.

He gave an imperceptible nod and looked as if he

was going to make a step towards us, but we had gone before he could move his second leg. Linda and I stifled our giggles and made our way right round the hall to stand next to the stage where there was such a squash of the group's fans that we had to elbow our way through to hide ourselves amongst them. The group was the Trekkers and although I rather liked one of them, their music held no magic for me. It was just loud. Another member of the group lived at the end of my road where his parents owned a nursery. I remember going to buy dahlias there for my Mum's birthday with money from my Dad. The colours dazzled and I probably chose a bunch of lurid ill matching blooms which I would nowadays heartily scorn. Anyway, this other Trekker member was one of the wood chompers for the local annual Bonfire Night. I remember being mortified one year when all the wood he and his mates had stacked up over several weeks stolen the night before the celebration. I think I may even have cried. I was only little and the fire was such an excitement.

Everyone came from around the neighbourhood bringing their own fireworks and treacle toffee and parkin. The pile had been growing steadily as I saw it each day on my way to and from school and my excitement had been growing with it. But on the morning of that Bonfire Night when I went past, I felt as bereft as a child can be. Most of the wood had gone. I looked at the pitiful remains and couldn't imagine how anyone could have removed it. That was vandalism in my day! But somehow, our chompers got more wood from somewhere and we had our Bonfire Night after all. I remember the relief and happiness of it. The lads probably went and stole their own wood back, recognising it on some other local pile. I thought they were wonderful.

THREE

I called for Linda the next Monday. Usually she was ready for me, but if not, it was her mother who came to the door. Today, the stony face of the Reverend looked down upon me, making me feel like the sinner that I undoubtedly was. He may have been the kindest father in the world, but to me he was 'the vicar', a dark and intimidating figure, who made me almost swallow my tongue with the anxiety of what to say. Actually, I didn't say anything but stood there allowing him to guess why I was positioned outside his front door with the twisted face of a turtle.

Linda's mother always made me think of a farmer's wife. She had a gentle voice and the rosy face I thought all farmer's wives ought to have. All that fresh air and fresh cream had made her face rounded and dimpled and then slipped south to meet her mid dle. I wasn't calling her fat. She wasn't fat. I don't know where her fresh cream had come from! Her plumpness was of the cosy sort and seemed made for consoling and comforting. She didn't seem to fit with the Reverend. They seemed an odd pair to me. I thought Linda looked a bit like her mother. She was a bit on the plump side too and had the same beaming smile and soft brown hair. Me, I was skinny, skinny like a bean pole, with thin and stringy greasy hair. I only have one photo of us together, taken after we'd been on a church procession and I hope for both our sakes that I can't find it again. We look like gawky teenagers. Probably because that's what we were.

Anyway, that day, I didn't have to speak. Linda came tripping down the hall and claimed me. She found her Dad frowning and must have recognised the signs of an impending interrogation. He had no chance. She was ready for him. 'Where are you off to?' The Reverend's voice was loud and emphatic, like he was just about to explode into a sermon. I prepared myself for an announcement regarding the angry hell fire that was most definitely awaiting me. Linda was all innocent smiles.

'First to get an ice-cream and then for a walk.'

And all the Reverend did was nod. I smiled and nodded too, confirmation of Linda's words. If Linda was being evasive, she was not lying. A vicar's daughter would not lie. She just hadn't said where the walk would be taking us. The reverend didn't get time to ask that. We were off and down the road before the vicarage door closed, unknowing, behind us.

We walked briskly through the modern section of the cemetery. If we walked faster than usual, neither of us mentioned it. We understood each other. We did not want to meet our young gravedigger. We wanted to get from the main gates to our hidden spot without hindrance. I knew Linda was feeling my own embarrassment. We had snaked our way around that dance hall as if close contact with the grave digging lad would have been a contamination, though neither of us really knew why we felt such discomfort. We would have blushed to have been caught now, licking ice creams like babies. The girls' secondary schools we both attended did not include lessons on how to talk to the opposite sex without shifting your feet and looking steadfastly at the ground. We led lives isolated from the males of our species and, although we liked looking at them as through the bars of their cages, we did not want to come face to face with them and their bared teeth out in the open. We made it to the security of our old grave and relaxed into the last licks of our cornets.

'I've been thinking,' I began.

'Painful?' said Linda. It was an old joke and not even groan worthy.

'I thought I might borrow some of my Dad's gardening tools and try and tidy up the grave a bit. It was quite nice when we first came but as it's been so dry, it's all getting pretty messy. Look at all these dandelion clocks!'

'But all the other graves here are just the same. This one will look odd if you clear all the weeds. People will know that someone's been here.'

'I know, but I just feel I want to do something.'

'Yes, it's a bit sad that all these people have been

forgotten. And we have flattened all the grass out just sitting on it. They'll know someone's been here anyway.'

'It'll just go back to the state it was in before when we have to go back to school. Or are you going to come and see to it all through the winter too?'

'I don't expect so. I won't be coming here on my own in the dark, that's for sure. Far too creepy in the dark.'

'Well then, what's the point?'

I didn't know then that I was going to be-come a keen gardener in my later life. I'd never helped in the garden at home. I'd never even mowed a lawn. I didn't know the difference between plants and weeds except that gardeners seemed to want to encourage the first and eliminate the latter. I had simply assumed that all the plants growing on the grave were weeds and perhaps it was some sort of latent instinct that made me want to get rid of them?

'Well, please yourself. I suppose I could help. I don't know if we have any garden tools at home that

I could borrow though.'

'You have a garden. Someone must look after it. But it doesn't matter. I'm quite happy to do it. You can just keep me company. After all, it's not exactly Buckingham Palace is it? Not even the size of a real garden. It's really no bigger than a sand pit.'

My Dad kept his gardening tools in the wash-house, mainly because when I was younger I had taken over the garden shed. I regularly took everything out of the shed, the big items, my parents' bikes, the old pram, the old mower, every item I found there, and dumped them somewhere in the back drive and then set up house inside the now empty wooden hut. Dad couldn't have minded too much as he'd put up a little wooden cupboard inside for me and I used a battered, ancient trunk as a bed, with the old black-out curtains as covers. I'd not known that they were black-out curtains at first. They were my mother's. Mum had lived in rented rooms in Liverpool during the war and had often talked about looking out to watch the bombs dropping over the docks every night. The fires had burned long into the darkness. She'd held the black-out curtains tight as she watched, trying to keep the light in, but had once been told off by a look-out warden. Now, the curtains were covered in paint splodges, mainly white and magnolia, as my Dad used them to cover the furniture when he was deco-rating. I sometimes made dens with them too, using the bars of my swing in the garden for supports.

Dad came out as I was rooting around for garden-ing tools and I had to confess what I was up to. He suggested a trowel. A spade would be an encum-brance, he said, to carry off to the cemetery. I had to promise to bring the trowel back though, no leaving it there for the next day.

Otherwise, he didn't seem too worried about his daughter traipsing about in a cemetery. He told me to stick with Linda and worry more about real live men than dead ones. He didn't believe in ghosts and repeated his old story about a white shape hovering over a bridge on the Nab, what the locals called the open countryside beyond Chorley, where he'd been brought up. He went camping there a lot as a lad with his friend Owen Griffiths, who'd never come back from the war. He'd gone somewhere exotic and I later liked to think of him as disappearing whilst working on something like the bridge over the River Kwai. I could see that in my imagination. Anyway, Dad had gone off alone to a farm one late evening to get some milk when on one of those camping trips. The bridge was supposed to be haunted by some eerie lady who regularly drifted across it in long, floaty, white garments. That evening, the lady had duly appeared and my father had stood transfixed to the ground with his heart beating double, unable to move, unable to run. However, when Dad heard the floaty white spectre mooing, he forgot his previous caution and breezed across, just skirting the stately 'lady' and giving her a friendly pat.

Linda had brought some secateurs. I didn't say anything but wondered what she could do with those on our grave. She began by cutting the dandelions down by their stems, one at a time, and winced when she saw me just digging them up whole alongside her. Realising the error, she discreetly sidled off and I next saw her hacking overgrown stems down on neighbouring graves, shrubs and rose bushes which had become shapeless thugs. She was also sucking thorns from her fingers. But she was removing the branches which made up our hide-way screen. Without them, we would be exposed to the world and the whole idea of our retreat would be lost.

It took me a while to pluck up the courage to tell her to stop and point out that we needed those long stems. Then she pouted.

'Well, what do you want me to do?'

'I'm not in charge. Do what you want.'

Actually, she had also brought some old newspapers along. That proved to be a brilliant idea. She began piling up the weeds I'd removed onto the open newspaper pages and then scooped everything up to take it all to one of the bins. Meanwhile, I made good progress. My Dad had told me about

S.DAVEY

couch grass, how that if I left the tiniest strand of root behind, the plant would simply grow again and all the time I had spent extracting it would be wasted. I became intrigued by tracing the roots back through the soil to their origins and feeling jubilant when I re-moved long threads of the stuff. It was as if I were warring against the couch grass and tracing the roots back through the soil to each dangling string was a battle won.

I was so absorbed in my fight that I didn't notice that Linda had been gone quite a while after her first short reconnaissance trip. Suddenly anxious and remembering my Dad's words, I stood up quickly. There was Linda, returning and beaming all over her face. I was strangely annoyed. Her absence had frightened me, even though it had taken me ages to notice it. The Great White Slave Traders could have had her and been long gone. Better to feel irritated with her than guilty about myself.

'I met Dennis,' she announced.

'Dennis?' I didn't want to encourage her.

She was evidently very pleased with herself but, even as I asked, I knew who she was referring to. She would love it that she had got in first.

'The gravedigger.'

'The young one?'

'Yes, how did you know?'

'It's grinning all over your face. I can't imagine you with a face like that after meeting Old Joe and Old Bill'.

'He's rather nice. Even in his old togs. And the old ones aren't called Joe and Bill either.'

I waited for the revelation. Her silence ladled out her superiority. She knew some-thing I didn't and she wanted to make me wait. Maddened, I knelt down and returned to my weeding.

'Don't you want to know their names?'

'If you want to tell me.'

We had played this game so many times. It was who could hang on the longest.

Linda made a big gesture of gathering up some more of the weeds I had unearthed during her trip to the bins. As she set off to get rid of them, she turned round and called back … 'Joe and Arnold.'

So, I had guessed correctly for one of the names. She wouldn't have liked that and by flouncing off to the bins, she was removing my chance to point it out. When she got back, she sat down beside me and waited for me to say something. But the couch grass fascinated me … it still does when I have to renovate a patch of the stuff … that she eventually had to open the conversation.

'Don't you want to know about him?'

'Who, old Arnold?'

'Oh, stop it! You're just being awkward!'

Actually, I did want to know about this Dennis, even if Linda had bagged him first. First seeing gets first chance. That was the rule. Not that either of us had nabbed anyone so far.

'He's not a real gravedigger. The other two are, but he goes to the Catholic College. He's going into the Lower Sixth at the end of the holidays. So, he's just doing a holiday job.'

'I've never heard of grave digging as a holiday job. How did he get that?'

'His uncle got it for him. He's something to do with the management of cemeteries in Preston ... the uncle I mean. They're wanting to tidy up the over-grown parts of the old section and basically are do-ing what we're doing, clearing out all the rubbish and weeds, revealing the headstones. They just start-ed at the other side to us.'

'I've seen them digging graves.'

'Yes, well that's when a grave is required. He helps with all the normal stuff gravediggers do as well. He says he'll come and see what we're up to sometime. Not today though. They're opening up a grave for a funeral tomorrow.'

'In the old section?'

'No, but he saw me at the bins and came up to say hello. He saw us at the Youth Club dance. He knew it was us.'

'He must think we're a bit daft. How many other young people would lark about in a cemetery for their summer holidays?'

'He does.'

'Yes, but he's getting paid.'

'And he said to come across to see them sometime as well.'

'I don't want to go visiting today. I don't want to see inside an uncovered grave.'

'Mmm,'said Linda, 'we'd see the coffins below. Maybe we'd see through the wood which had rotted in the damp? Maybe we'd see some bleached white bones? Maybe there'd be …'I could see her imagination was ready to take flight. She'd got that look on her. I stopped her before I began to feel ill.

'I don't think you get bleached bones in a coffin that's been underground for a while. Isn't it the sun that does the bleaching? Someone who's died of thirst in the desert perhaps? You know the sort of thing … Beau Geste, is it? '

'I take your point. What would the damp do to a corpse then?'

'I've no idea. It's not something I've studied

64

recently. Nothing pleasant, I should think. White mould perhaps? Now, look! I've nearly finished. How do you think it looks?'

I thought I'd done a pretty good job. The weeds were all gone. There were no huge clods of earth. I had hoed away with the end of the trowel and neatened everything up.

I was quite pleased with my first gardening assignment. Linda must have recognised my self-satisfaction shining through. I could see her preparing to strike.

'Very tidy. A bit sad though.'

'What do you mean, sad?'

Linda's head cocked to one side. I could tell that this was the moment when she'd get her own back. For the ill use of the secateurs, for my bone corrections, for my apparent lack of interest in her seeing Dennis first. She was sifting through the thesaurus, which was her brain, to find a whole host of words to put me in my place.

'It looks bereft. So different from all the other

graves around it. Dark, black soil. No greenery. Desolate, forlorn, cheerless, full of woe.'

'That's enough. You been writing poetry again?'

Linda smiled. Over sweetly.

'So, what do you suggest we do about this poor, dejected looking grave, then?'

'It needs a vase with some flowers in. Well, a jam jar at least. You got any flowers in that garden of yours?'

Back home that evening, Dad let me take some blue flowers he called 'Love in a Mist'. He said to refresh the water now and again but leave the flowers to set seed. The seed heads would be as pretty as the flowers. We could have them in a jam jar in lieu of flowers and after a while, the seed heads wouldn't even need water and we could put them in a jar and leave them for the rest of the year. Winter decorations dealt with! The seed heads would burst and would set more plants for next year. It sounded too good to be true.

Years later, I now wonder if that part of the

cemetery is overgrown with 'Love in a Mist' flowers.

We never went back to visit our grave after that first
year and Linda and I eventually went our separate
ways as we grew up. I have no idea where she is
now or what happened to her. It's sad that we lose
friends and family to life and the passing of time.
'Love in a Mist' plants certainly crop up all over the
place in my own garden. One packet of seeds care-
lessly cast forth one spring has produced no end of
babies in spite of all my attention. The seedlings
hide so well.

That summer's day I also brought some rosettes of
something called 'London Pride' from my parents'
garden. Apparently, all I had to do was press the rosettes into the soil and they would eventually take
over the whole of the grave area. They didn't need
watering and they would clear out the weeds in their
path too. The flowers were not impressive but they
had the advantage of being free. Linda brought a
plant she called 'White Rock'. She said that it was

all they had in their back garden. She said it was everywhere. We planted our meagre collection the next day and set the flowers in a jam-jar. We had both brought one and so we stripped some of the 'White Rock' flowers off the plants and had a jar of 'Love in a Mist' at the head of the grave and a jar of 'White Rock' at the feet. The plants were watered copiously in. They were given far more water than they probably needed since Linda insisted on going for water so many times in the hope, I suspected, of seeing Dennis at the tap. She was repeatedly disappointed and the plants also looked pretty sorry for themselves when we left to go home. Now, I understand that moving plants in summer is decidedly the wrong thing to do. But, we hoped that they would perk up overnight and, equally hopeful, Linda declared that, given the names of the plants, our grave was a very poetic one … Love in a Mist, London Pride and White Rock. Perhaps she thought that it symbolised something to come for her and Dennis. I could tell she was quite taken with him now that she knew he was not a real grave digger. Now she could look past the grubby and worn working clothes he wore. For my part, though I thought he was quite good looking, I felt she was on a hiding to nothing if the Reverend father ever discovered that Linda's new love interest was a Catholic. I don't think that had dawned on her yet. Linda also seemed to have forgotten all about poor, or not so poor, Dave Appleton. After all the time we had spent discussing him too. Instead, Linda was impressed with the romance of the 'Love in a Mist', an illustrious omen she thought, and she was a tad disappointed when I told her its official name was actually Nigella. That didn't sound half as lyrical. I've since looked up the names of the other plants. She would probably have liked London Pride. Not so much Saxifraga Urbian, but its other more common name of 'Look up and Kiss me.' Unfortunately, White Rock is not so impressive. It turned out to be Dover Clover, a form of clover. No romance there!

FOUR

I was surprised to find myself looking forward to seeing how the newly planted rosettes and rock plants had gone on overnight in our grave garden. Would the coolness of the darkness have effected a refreshing resuscitation? But all that flowery stuff went out of my head as soon as we arrived at the graveside. I don't think there was anything in Linda's head either as we stood there together looking down at the work we had done the day before. We were both speechless. There was that boy I mentioned earlier, just lying before us on the grave-mound. This was the first time we saw him. All the plants we had set into the soil had been squashed under his body. Were they dead? A flash of anger sped through me as I thought of the lack of consideration in the lad. What sort of person lies down on plants that have so obviously just been bedded in and tended? Then, I thought of how wet he must be lying on that well and truly watered ground. Both the jam-jars had been knocked over and he was half

70

sitting, half lying on the flowers they had contained and in the water that had poured from them. One of the jars was wedged underneath his semi prone back. How could he not notice the discomfort of it pinned into his side? He was lying in a lazy kind of way against the tombstone and both his eyes were closed. I remember wondering whether he was sleeping or whether his eyes were just closed against the sun which had decided to appear through the clouds after a morning of mist. Linda and I stood on in silence. I had no idea what to say and supposed that Linda must be feeling much like me. Out of all the graves in the old section why had this boy chosen to settle himself on what we now considered 'ours'? Wouldn't he have been more far comfortable on a grave layered with grass and which had dried out over the summer? Whereas, now, his clothes must have been sodden beneath him and his flesh in danger of being pierced with shards of glass as his weight might at any moment shatter the jam jar.

I saw Linda shrug and look at me. We neither of us

knew what to do. It was as if our private space had been violated. All we wanted was to get rid of him and continue with our gossiping, our pottering, our usual afternoon activities. It wasn't as if the lad was good looking and an attractive find for two teenage girls. He was pasty faced and lifeless. There was no promise of laughter or joking in him. He was a wet rag and the sooner we could move him, the better.

We both realised that we had no idea how we were going to do that. I coughed; I thought he might have been asleep, but there was no movement. For a moment I wondered if we might have discovered a dead body but somehow I knew we hadn't. Linda coughed more loudly and I saw the boy's eyelids flutter slightly. And so we both coughed together. Very very loudly. If we hadn't been a bit scared, we might have collapsed into silly laughter. We were both more than a little bewildered. But then, as we watched the boy's eyes opened slightly and then widened before us. There was no fear in them, just a look of passing surprise that soon settled into passive stillness. There was no curiosity in him. We, on the other hand, were very curious about him, as much as we were anxious, but he was clearly not the slightest bit interested in us.

'What are you doing here?' I asked, as if he were a burglar I had just discovered in my living room. I probably didn't sound very friendly.

There was no reply, though he did shuffle his body into more of a sitting position against the tomb stone. In his position, I would have been fiddling distastefully with my wet trousers and pulling the jam-jar out from where it had now lodged under my buttocks. But he was not looking at us anymore. He was back in his previous dozy state.

'What are you doing here?' Linda repeated.

'Nothing,' he said. We had to lean forward. It was as if he had a mouthful of damp gravel. His answer was pretty accurate. Nothing. He was just lying there as if there was nothing of interest to him in the world.

There had been a slow girl just like him in my class

at primary school. I suppose we'd call her special needs now but then we had no such kind terms. We just thought that she was just dopey, or worse. We weren't particularly cruel back then and no one ever hurt her or called her names. At least I never heard or saw anything. We mostly just ignored her. We had tried to be friendly when she first joined the class. She could walk around like the rest of us and she ate her school dinner with a mechanical sort of interest, but there was no life in her. There was 'no one at home' as some of my classmates said about her. This boy was just like that. I tried again.

'Where have you come from?'

'Over there.'

There was no pointing. It was just an answer. We were no better off.

'Over there' signified nothing. I helped him out.

'Is it over there?' I pointed away to the front of the grave.

There was the merest movement of his head. I took it for no. Linda, cottoning on, tried again, pointing to the other side this time. The same head movement. My turn again.

'Is it that way?'

This was the opposite side. Linda and I didn't know our easts from our wests or whatever, except perhaps on a map that was the 'right' way up. The last direction pointed away to behind the headstone. The boy nodded. Maybe it was a truthful answer or may-be he had just realised that he was running out of directions. Linda and I looked at one another. There was no way out behind. There was just that high stone wall.

We had explored the cemetery in every direction when we'd first spent time there. There were official entrances at either end of the place and then you could get out unofficially on the other side by climb-ing over the low wall there. At one time this wall had clearly had high metal railings confining the cemetery space. It had metal stumps all along its length now, like badly overgrown and stumpy teeth.

We guessed the metal had been removed to help

the war effort. The railings had been taken away to be turned into armaments, trains, aeroplanes and so on. We knew quite a lot about the war. The

memory of it was still fresh in most of the adults around us and the baddies in all the films and in my brother's comics were always Germans. But for the moment, the question Linda and I were both asking ourselves was how had this boy come from the direction of the wall? He would have had to climb it. Maybe he hadn't even realised that there was a wall there. Maybe he had come in overnight in the dark? We had cornered him in and he had to accept with a nod.

'You climbed in then? Over the wall?'

Another vague nod. I think we both felt a strange satisfaction that we had him scuppered. We looked at him with smug satisfaction, knowing that there was no way he could have climbed over that wall.

Certainly not in the state he now was. He seemed to have no muscles, no energy in him to get up from where he lay, never mind climb such a high wall.

We examined it again. It was as sound as we had first thought, with no loose stones or gaps of missing mortar for any footholds. We didn't see how anyone could get over it. Maybe with ropes and whatever else rock climbers use, but not this flimsy bit of a lad. I felt a strong urge to go in for the kill and let him know that we knew he was lying. There was no need for the lying. What was he trying to hide? I didn't like him for it. Actually, there was something a bit distasteful about him altogether. I could see he was going to smash those jam-jars, either with his foot or by just moving his upper body, but I couldn't bring myself to lean forward and move them out of his way. I didn't want my hand to catch even a part of his clothing. I could feel myself grimacing at the thought of it, my lips pinching as I imagined the wetness of his underwear and the dirtiness of the soil clinging to him. I'd had my hands in that soil the day before but now it was somehow contaminated. Maybe Linda felt as I did but perhaps she, with her holier background, was stirring with some of that religious virtue that she had absorbed at her father's knee? She was probably beginning to feel sorry for him. Or would she kick me later for even thinking that? She did not like being tarred with a holy brush.

'Are you OK? Do you feel ill? Can we help you with something?'

Too many questions at once probably.

As if we were flaying him alive with whips, the boy shuddered and turned his head away from us and we could see he had closed his eyes again. I couldn't help thinking what a wimp he was.

'I know you can still hear us,' I said. I was trying not to be too aggressive but maybe I sounded so to him? I softened my voice. 'What's your name?'

He turned back. There was even a hint of a smile across his mouth.

'Jack'.

Linda and I introduced ourselves. I felt silly even as I spoke. He had shown no interest in us. He should have had his own questions. But Linda persevered.

'Do you live round here?'

There was no answer and the eyes closed once more. I guessed it was his way of avoiding questions he didn't want to answer.

He wasn't going to give anything away and why should we worry about him? But Linda wasn't quite ready to give in.

'Do you need us to help you get home? You seem ill.'

A garbled voice grunted at us. Those pebbles were grating again in his mouth and we couldn't make anything out. We stretched forward to hear better. Maybe he was just reluctant to speak to us? Maybe he was sleeping off a hangover? Not that I knew anything much about hangovers but I'd seen people with them on T.V. I knew they came from drinking too much alcohol, but the boy looked much too young for that.

'No. Just tired'. At least, that's what we thought he'd said. We could just have been hearing what we wanted to hear.

'Shall we leave you alone?' This was me now. I'd had enough of him. He had spoilt our afternoon and stolen our chosen spot in the cemetery. He'd ruined the work I'd done on the grave. I just couldn't be bothered with him anymore.

'Should we tell someone you're here?'

For the first time, the boy, Jack, spoke loudly and clearly. Though it was only one word.

'No,' and he repeated it several times. He was the one beginning to sound aggressive now. I didn't like it and took several steps away from the graveside. He didn't want us and I certainly didn't want him.

'Come on,' I said to Linda. 'We need to leave him. This is just a waste of time.'

'Bye, Jack,' Linda turned and moved al-most re-luctantly away and followed me back to the main avenue through the cemetery. I was striding out well ahead of her. I shouted a goodbye of my own but it was only because I was copying her.

We hardly spoke on the way back. Linda wondered if we ought to report him to someone. I think she meant the grave diggers, though we hadn't seen them anywhere that afternoon. I said she was making a fuss. He'd said he wasn't ill. He didn't want our help.

'Maybe he was just drunk. I couldn't smell any alcohol. Wasn't he a bit young to be drinking?' She was thinking just like I had earlier.

I shrugged. How would I know? I didn't really know what alcohol smelt like. My parents had a cupboard full of bottles but they were never touched, except at Christ-as, and even then, only if someone visited. Linda was making me feel guilty and that was making me bad tempered. She was anxious about the lad but I just wanted to get away from him. He was creepy, but mostly I was just angry with him. If he was ill, he should have said so.

We didn't fall out properly but even so, it was clear the afternoon was at an end. We both just wanted to go home. I felt that home was somewhere where I wouldn't be questioned, where I wouldn't have any doubts about myself, where I wouldn't feel that I had let Linda down, let the boy down. I was angry that he should have made me feel like that.

But home was not as restful as I had thought. I spent the rest of the evening worrying about whether I had been uncaring. Really, I knew I had been. I had done First Aid at Guides and at school and then, at the first sign of trouble, I had not been able to get away fast enough. I was hoping that Linda would be as kind to me as she'd been with that boy. We had agreed to meet to go back to the cemetery the next day but I couldn't help wondering if she'd seen what a mean character I could be at times and wouldn't want to be friends anymore. And I prayed that the boy would be OK. We, especially me, could be in an awful lot of trouble if he'd died after we'd left.

FIVE

It was such a relief to see Linda coming towards me down Stuart Road the next afternoon.

'I didn't know whether you would still want to come after yesterday. So, I thought I'd come and collect you.' She was smiling anxiously.

I didn't throw my arms around her but I felt as if I could have done. She looked equally glad to see me.

'I was horrid yesterday,' I said. 'I'm sorry.'

'It was all horrid yesterday. What a strange boy! I couldn't make him out. I hope he's gone.'

I hoped the same so much that I was jittery all the way to the graveside. Linda seemed twitchy too. There was nothing to be said between us. It was as if we had gritted our teeth to stride off positively together and yet the nearer we got to the spot, the slower we became, until, when, only a few yards away from the place, still hidden from our view by overgrown bushes, we were scarcely moving forward at all. There wasn't a sound coming from the grave, but then what sound would the lad have made? We almost leaned our way towards the grave and peered ahead. He wasn't there. I almost cheered. He wasn't dead. I hadn't deserted a dying boy. I could hear Linda's intake of breath beside me. We had been so quiet that even our breath now sounded loud. We had probably both held our breath those last few moments. I hadn't been able to hear myself breathe, never mind Linda. The world had stopped.

We both moved nearer. The jam-jars were lying just as they had been the day before. They were not smashed, nor had he straightened them. The flowers looked crushed but the London Pride rosettes had held their place. I took both jars and set them up round the back of the tombstone. I have no idea why I did that. Was it so that he couldn't sit on them again if he came back? I hoped he wasn't going to come back. Why should he, after all?

There was nothing special about 'our' grave, except that we had cleared it. Now, I felt compelled to

wash my hands, as if the jars had somehow contaminated me. I shoved the Love in a Mist flowers,
squashed though they were, into one of the jars but
they would be waterless from now on. Linda did
the same with the White Rock. They were no longer pretty offerings to our special spot. I thought of
my father's words and wondered whether they
might just survive.

'I'm going to wash my hands at the tap,' I said
without explanation.

'I'm coming with you.'

Obviously neither of us wanted to be on our own
if the boy were to reappear.

I rubbed and rubbed at my hands under the cold
water tap. There was obviously no soap, but I felt
that the rubbing would make me feel better. Linda
watched without comment and then as I shook
them dry she said

'I don't want to go back there. At least not today.
What about you?'

'I don't either, but I have an idea. Why don't we

walk out of the cemetery at the other end and through to where the other side of the wall would be. Let's check his story out.'

I don't know why I wanted to follow the boy's tale through but something about him had intrigued me. The whole thing had been weird. Now that I knew he wasn't dead, I was annoyed with him again. There was something wrong and I didn't like being messed about. I didn't say anything to Linda but I think she must have understood. She set off at once and I had to run to catch her up, as if having made a decision, there was to be no dithering.

We had to leave the cemetery through the gates at the opposite end to those we had come through earlier. We were out on the main road which now leads down to the M6 motorway. I can't remember if the motorway was there then. When did motor ways join the world? We turned left. I'd rarely been this way before but I knew roughly where we were as there was a school for the blind across the road a little further on. My Dad had a friend who was the headmaster there and we'd once been for tea and a look round, Dad and me, when I was younger. Dad had gone hiking with this friend all around the Black Forest in Germany when I was about two years old. I still had the scar on my chin from when I'd fallen on a nail during his absence and, in a panic, my Mum hadn't known what to do. She hadn't dare ring for an ambulance, perhaps not thinking it was serious enough for that, and we'd no car then. She couldn't have driven one in any case. She never passed her test. I probably should have had a stitch or two but I survived and no one ever notices it now, though the mark is still there if you know where to look.

The road to the motorway sloped down-wards and I seem to remember some three bed semis and the occasional bungalow on the left hand side. Their gardens grew steeper as the gradient downhill increased. Mowing a lawn would have been impossible and they'd all been terraced or turned into sloping rockeries. We turned off left before them

into the road we guessed ran alongside the cemetery on our grave's side. There were more three bed
semis and then they petered out and we could see
the high wall behind our grave through the car park
of what looked to be some offices and a warehouse. We were even brave enough to wander into
the car park to get a closer look. We expected to be
shooed off at any moment, ears ready for an en-
raged cry. But no one came or shouted from a window, though it did feel as if eyes were fixed upon
us waiting to see if we were going to become little
vandals. The wall went right along the back of the
warehouse and we could see that it continued further on along the backs of people's gardens. It must
have been the original wall to the cemetery. We
didn't dare go clambering into the gardens, but we
could see that the wall continued at the back as far
as we could see. The most important thing was that
it was obviously not a wall anyone could easily
climb over and certainly not a wasted, limp lad
with no apparent muscles. There were no toe or

hand holds on this side either. We both had a little try, conscious of those eyes upon us and then cleared out as fast as we could.

We did talk on the way back. It was as if our tongues had been suddenly loosened and needed to catch up.

'So, where did he go last night?' I began. 'He couldn't have climbed the wall. I don't think he could even have walked very far. The houses we've just seen are the nearest ones and I don't think he could have got to any of those on foot.'

'Perhaps he had escaped from the blind school and just got lost. He didn't seem to see us when he looked in our direction, did he? Perhaps he was blind? He had that glassy eyed look you sometimes see on the blind. Perhaps people came looking for him? They could shout out for him, couldn't they? He would have been able to hear them and shout back.'

'And they took him away again after we'd left.'

It seemed the most obvious explanation but I

couldn't seem to shake off the idea that he'd been ill. That pale, insipid face was not a healthy one. He had scarcely been able to talk to us. How could he have been able to shout to his rescuers? I still felt a trickle of guilt running through me for leaving him that I needed to wipe away. Especially if he'd been blind.

'Or, the gravediggers could have found him. I've forgotten their names, apart from your friend Dennis.'

'He's not my friend. I hardly know him. Joe and Arnold. Anyway, what would they have done with him?'

'I don't know. Called the Police or maybe an ambulance. That's why he's gone. One of those came to fetch him. Or all of them. He looked as if he needed some sort of help.'

'Well, if that's the case, we should ask them.'

'The Police?'

'No, idiot, Joe and Arnold.'

'Don't forget your friend Dennis.'

'He's not …..' But, decision made, she was off again, with me trailing behind as usual.

Linda found the gravediggers straightaway. It was as if she had her own internal radar. She homed in on everything. I was the one who missed whatever was going on, too busy formulating plans of my own. Daydreaming you might say. I still do it. Linda found Joe and Arnold fast enough. At least she found two men who I assumed were Joe and Arnold. The evidence of their digging was all around them, piled up into a sizeable mound. They were, in fact, sitting on it, drinking from old china mugs.

'Ah, ladies', one said. 'You must be our Dennis's lady friends.'

We supposed we were. We were flattered that Dennis must have spoken about us.

'Come for some tea, have you? You chose the right time. You can borrow young Dennis's mug. He's not here at the moment.' He picked up a flask that had been standing near him.

Linda's face did not shift, even though I knew she

had grabbed this excuse to come looking for him. Dennis's absence would be a disappointment.

'Where is he then?'

'Well, it's a manner of speaking,' said the other. 'He's not here with us, but he is really.'

His partner was giggling. Do old codgers giggle? We must have just looked confused.

'Stop teasing, Joe. You're such a leg-puller.'

'Just having a bit of fun. No 'arm in it.'

At that moment, the sound of loud banging came from just alongside us. Linda and I both jumped and the two men nearly choked themselves on gulps of tea.

'Oops, the ghosts are out again.' It was the leg puller grinning.

Linda and I leaned over to look in the grave the men had been preparing. Thank goodness it was a new one. There were no coffins to see but we did see the top of Dennis's head bobbing up and down as he banged away at some planking. It was deep down there, much deeper than I had imagined and

all the earth on the sides was shored up with more
of the wooden planks that Dennis was fixing into
place.

'You get down there and you can't hear a thing'
explained Arnold. 'Just the sound of your own
noise ringing around your head.'

'You can't always get out again either.'

Joes shrugged. 'Just have to leave people down
there when that happens. Maybe that'll be young
Dennis's fate.'

Linda and I both leaned further forward to call to
Dennis. My feet were firmly rooted to the ground.
There was no way I was going to risk toppling
over. But as I peered over the edge, the smell of
deep earth hit my nostrils. It wasn't like the smell
of the soil on the grave which I had just spent two
days turning over. That soil had had a clean fresh-
ness to it. It had reminded me of muzzy rain on an
autumn day, waiting for the mist to lift and the sun
to find its way through the clouds. This new smell
was the smell of a musty room, where there had

been no new air for months. The autumn was in it but now the leaves had begun to mould, turn blue-green and white in the damp atmosphere. The dankness of it seeped through me. I could feel it in my clothes. I could feel it sinking through into my body. And straight away I recognised it. It was the smell that had clung to that boy. It had been in his clothes and had crept out from him into the air around him, into my waiting nostrils. I tried to catch Linda's eye. As she looked across, I inhaled deeply, though God knows I didn't want to. I didn't want that smell penetrating through me again, but I had to get Linda to notice. I kept my mouth tightly shut as if that made a difference. I tried to cock my head slightly towards the grave as I did so. It was a message to make her take note of the smell. I didn't know whether she had understood or not until we both stood up and she gave the smallest nod you could possibly give, a little sign of acknowledg-ment which told me she'd smelt it too. I was trying to take great gulps of fresh air as I moved away from the graveside and couldn't join her in shouting for Dennis. She must have had a stronger stomach than I did.

But Arnold had noticed.

'You alright, girl? It's the grave smell. You gets used to it. Does no harm. You'll soon be over it.'

Joe couldn't let the occasion pass. 'It's better with a coffin or two inside. The smell is sweeter then.'

'I can tell you enjoy your job.' That was me, trying to make light of the moment. It was not how I felt.

'Well, you has to laugh,' said Arnold. 'It's a cheerless thing to work for the dead. And we are working for them. It's the relatives as pay, but it's the dead who draws us here. We gravediggers need to have a bit of fun now and again, don't we? Couldn't do the job otherwise. But that's enough, Joe. You can see the girl's a bit shaken up.'

I could hardly imagine what 'fun' there was working in a cemetery but the two old men looked happy enough.

By this time, Dennis had heard Linda and was scrambling up over the top soil. He made it look effortless. How long had he been working here to be able to do that with so much ease?

'Hey, what are you two doing here? Come visiting after all?'

'We offered them a bit of tea. But we'd have to use your mug. You wouldn't have minded, would you?'

The thought of drinking out of a mug that had been touched previously by hands that had delved in that earth was sick making. I saw Linda's nose shrink like mine. We declined as fast as possible.

'Actually, we came to ask for your help,' Linda began.

'Help? I don't know as we'd be any help to two young girls like you.'

That was Joe but they were all three sitting up with interest now. Dennis had joined Joe and Arnold on the earth piles. Linda and I were not going to sit on any of that earth. We both realised that it

96

was the earth which had come from down there. It was bad enough standing nearby. Its smell was still percolating through me.

'Have you seen a young lad around here recently? Looking a bit ill perhaps? Looking as if he could do with a bit of help getting about?' Linda seemed unaffected by the rank odour. She obviously did have a stronger stomach. Or less imagination.

'Did you find a lad lying on one of the graves last night?' I decided to be more specific. I didn't want to listen ad nauseam to tales of people walking their dogs or lads on a short cut through the place. I wanted to get away.

'Well, I don't think we forgot to bury any-one,' said Joe, 'and left him lying around for the night.' He was grinning again, pleased with himself and looked to his fellow for confirmation that he was a bit of a wag.

'So, you didn't need to ring for an ambulance for anyone? The police even?'

'Goodness! What 'ave we missed?' asked Arnold.

'The one time there's something interesting going on in this place and we're not here to see it.'

'No, it's nothing,' I said. I could see a long inter-rogation coming if I didn't bat it away now. 'It's just that we met a boy here last night who refused our help when we thought he looked ill. We both worried about him but when he wasn't here today, we hoped he'd got home safely.'

'He probably did,' Linda confirmed.

Well, he wasn't anything to do with us. Can't say as I saw a soul last night when I clocked off.'

'Me neither,' said Joe. And Dennis just shook his head. He was pouring tea out for himself from a grubby looking flask. Using his soil caked hands, which explained the dirtiness of the flask, along with the fact that it probably hadn't been washed in a long time. Thanks goodness we hadn't accepted any tea. I felt that if we didn't get away soon, my imagination would reach my stomach and I would be retching. I wondered if it was putting Linda off her new found Dennis? Worse than changing nappies when I'd done Child Nurse badge for Guides. I'd had to go to someone's house and look after this small child for an afternoon. Captain had set it up.

'Thanks anyway,' I said, still anxious to get away. This time, I set off first and Linda, who seemed as though she might have wanted to linger, had to chase after me.

'What's the hurry?'

'I didn't like that smell. It made me feel sick. I'm going to get an ice cream to take the taste of it away. Help me forget. I'll treat you. I think I've just enough money for one small one each.'

'I've got some money. Why don't we get a double?'

We sat on the low wall of a garden down Stuart Road on the way back to eat our ice creams and I think we avoided talking about what had happened. I didn't know what to make of that smell and I don't think Linda did either. Maybe it didn't mean anything? The feeling I had that it was somehow significant was just me daydreaming again.

Then, Linda said she couldn't come out the next day as they were having visitors and, in any case, it rained for the next two days and I didn't think about the cemetery at all after that. Then it was the weekend and it was only on Monday morning, nearly a week later, that Linda rang up to ask why I hadn't gone to church on Sunday and to the Sunday evening Youth Club. Had I been ill? I'd felt sick when we last talked but I'd eaten my ice cream enthusiastically enough. There was nothing wrong with me. I couldn't explain why. I just hadn't felt like going to either church or the Youth Club. Looking back now, I think I was beginning to move away from religion, beginning to question it all. But you can't easily say that to a vicar's daughter can you? And perhaps there was some fear in me about that strange boy. But why? He had nothing to do with going to church or to the Youth Club. Perhaps I was just being moody or there was something I wanted to watch on TV. I can't remember

now. In the end, we agreed to meet up in the afternoon and somehow we also ended up trooping
down the cemetery avenue en route to the grave.
Our feet seemed to just take us there. Or our curiosity? I know I wasn't convinced that I wanted to
carry on spending time there but I also felt that I
had to confirm that the lad would be seen no more.
I had to settle the thing in my head. I was optimis-
tic, confident and had shaken all concerns about the
boy out of my system during our time away from
the grave. I could tell Linda was the same. We
walked, we chatted, we never once faltered. The
shock was all the greater, then, when he was lying
there before us as we arrived. I heard myself gasp.
He looked much the same. He hadn't changed out
of those damp clothes. They still looked wet in
spite of the fact that the sun had returned with a
vengeance over the weekend after all that rain. He
did look a little more alert though. He was sitting
more upright, though he was still leaning against
the headstone. He turned slowly in our direction as

we arrived, but not with any recognition. I saw Linda try to smile as if she were an old friend.

'Hello, Jack. How are you today?'

No answer. Not even a smile. His eyes were dead. I thought again about the possibility that he was blind, as we'd considered.

'Where did you go the other day? We worried about you.' I still wanted an explanation.

We didn't get one. He turned away and then seemed to sit up more firmly, looking around him in every direction. He certainly had more about him than the last time, more energy. Not much more though. He was still sluggish and lifeless.

'Is Dolly here?'

Linda and I looked at one another in surprise. We had not expected a question from him. We were the ones asking the questions. And he was actually talking to us, which meant he must know that we were there. We looked back at him. Perhaps we were getting somewhere?

'Who is Dolly?'

He ignored that. He just repeated 'Is Dolly here?'

'No, she's not.' Linda had obviously decided to humour him.

'Where is she, then?'

'We don't know. Who is Dolly?'

'She's not here. I can't find her.'

'Where should we look for her? You tell us and we'll ty and find her.'

'She's not here. I can't find her.'

'Tell us where she should be.'

'She should be here. But she's not. I can't find her.'

I don't have Linda's patience. This was all a load of nonsense to me. How could we help him find this Dolly if he wouldn't tell us anything about her?

'Who is Dolly? What does she look like?'

'I can't find her. She's not here.'

'Did Dolly leave you here?'

'No. She came first. But she's not here.'

'Did she say she'd meet you here?'

'No, I thought she would be here. But I can't find

her.'

'Where do you live?'

'With Dolly. Where is she?'

'Tell us something about Dolly and then we could perhaps help you better.'

'She should be here.'

'Is Dolly your sister?'

'Yes. Where is she?'

This was going round in circles. Linda might have the patience for all this twisting and turning, but I didn't. The worst was that the boy was back in our lives. I didn't want him there, but I could tell Linda was being drawn in. In any case, he looked as if he was getting sleepy again. I hoped so, otherwise Linda would dance round and round him with questions and no real answers.

'I think we need to go now,' I said, as much to Linda as to the boy. 'We'll leave you to go home like the other day. Will you be OK?'

He turned away and closed his eyes as if we were no longer there.

'I must find Dolly.'

We tiptoed away. I certainly didn't want him waking up again.

'Do you think we ought to ask Dennis and the others to look out for him?'

I could feel myself getting anxious and yet I couldn't see what there was to be anxious about. It was my imagination again. I laughed. It sounded a nervous laugh to me but Linda didn't seem to notice. We were away from the grave now and I coughed loudly to send a ripple through my body to shake me out of this silly nonsense. Of course it was silly nonsense but I couldn't help the course my brain was taking.

'I think we should find them and get them to come back here with us to see this boy. I bet they'll just laugh at us. They'll be able to give us a perfectly acceptable explanation for him. Probably seen him before. He's probably just a local boy off school for the summer like us.'

So that is what we did. We found the grave

diggers filling in the grave they had been digging the last time. The flowers waiting to be put in place were beautiful. It's a pity we don't get to see the flowers people send to accompany our coffins. I certainly didn't expect to receive so many beautiful bouquets in my lifetime; one bunch at a time may-be for a birthday, an anniversary, but never so many at once. We have to be dead before we got them in quantity and then we are unable to appreciate them. Of course, the believers might be thinking that the dear deceased would be looking down from above and admiring the selection, see-ing who had sent what and so on. But I didn't believe that. I thought it was more likely that it was the mourners who would be doing the comparing and contrasting. They would have been reading the messages too, seeing who had sent what. But they might also have been noting who had not sent any-thing, or who had sent the meanest spray. Why else had I seen mourners touring the wreaths removed from the hearse to read the messages and the names? I don't think I was thinking all this as Linda and I trundled our way across the cemetery but I certainly think my experiences there that summer formed me in my later life. I'm still interested in the old graves but the flowers for me now are in my garden; not rustic heathers and sturdy conifers, the plants my husband likes. I love the perennials, the delicate faces, the pastel colours. And they come anew each year. That's the only

Resurrection I can understand.

Dennis, Joe and Arnold were there arranging bouquets and wreaths with all the aplomb of those who knew nothing about placing flowers together so that each collection might complement its neighbour. Not that the deceased would be worrying about that. The men seemed pleased to see us and immediately agreed to trot over to 'our' grave, as they put it, though there was no trotting, as in speed. I just knew the boy would be gone by the time they made it there.

Linda and Dennis strode ahead. I knew she was

feeling the same delay that was getting to me. Or perhaps she just wanted to home in on Dennis?

I kept pace with the elderly gentlemen, except that they probably weren't very elderly as they were still working. If they'd been old, they wouldn't have been able to dig those deep graves. Now retired people don't seem elderly to me, but perhaps people are taking care of themselves more?

When we arrived at our graveside we found Dennis and Linda just standing there and staring down hard at the burial mound. There was no sign of Jack.

'There's nothing there,' announced Joe when he joined them. He stuck his thumbs into his old waistcoat pockets as if there was nothing else to say. He was supposedly displaying the wisdom of the ages, but I was wondering where was the wisdom in wearing a waistcoat in a cemetery for working in the summer? Or in wearing a waistcoat at all?

'No-one' agreed Arnold. As if it needed

confirmation or he was correcting his mate's vocabulary. We *had* been talking about person, not a thing. A young lad.

'But you can see where he's been lying.' I pointed to the flattened plants and the wetness when the summer had been mostly dry. The wetness of the spilt jam-jars which hadn't been able to dry out with a body lying over the soil.

'Could be an animal kipping there at night?'

'But we've seen him.' Linda sounded bad tempered. As if she really wanted to tell the two gents how stupid they were. Or as if she was annoyed that Jack had disappeared just as we needed him.

'You could be mistaken.'

'I think we know the difference between an animal and a human being.'

'Well, there's nowt there now and it's nearly our break time. Shall we go for a cuppa?'

The diggers trundled off to their hut. It was a ramshackled wooden shed at the far exit to the cemetery where they kept their 'stuff' and where

109

they were allowed to shelter from the rain. If it was a really wet day, a storm or snow, I think they were allowed to go home. I don't know whether they still got paid though. And their work was hardly seasonal. People did keep on dying, probably more in the winter months because of the cold and wet. It must have been hard digging graves when the ground was frozen. There were flu and pneumonia epidemics and not everybody had central heating in those days. There would have been more deaths than ever. I remember our central heating being put in and the problems my parents had complained about to the owner of the plumbing company. The man had actually come to our house. He was Tommy Finney, a very famous footballer for Preston North End Football Team. Dad and my brother were delighted. Now, it seems no young lads have ever heard of him.

Joe and Arnold cherished the old shack as a cosy escape and had set themselves up with a kettle and their old, battered mugs. They could entertain themselves with a pack of cards or a game of dominos. I don't suppose there was much conversation to be had on the subject of graves and their digging? But I had heard talk of bacon butties and other delicacies.

Dennis had not said a word. I supposed he wanted to align himself with us but couldn't contradict his so called 'superiors'. After all he was 'nobbut a lad' according to them. In spite of the fact that he must have had some brains. Linda had told me he was wanting to study Medicine at university. More likely, he wanted to align himself with Linda, because he had taken to ignoring me and the pair of them were all chat.

'I accept that you must have seen something,' he was now saying, but Linda and I could both hear the 'but' coming and interrupted him in unison.

'Someone.'

'Well, yes. But could it have been your imagination?'

He must have felt us both bristling.

'Oh, yes.' I said, 'because we're female and our skulls are so cluttered with rubbish that we might just have got things in a muddle.'

'Yes, I hardly know whether it's day or night,' Linda agreed.

I think we must have started picking up the feminist vibes that were just beginning to hit the country, rolling in, I expect, from the USA. Marylyn Monroe had died a year or two back and there had been derogatory comments about her alongside the praise. She'd been just a man's plaything, a simpering and brainless blonde. She'd caused trouble on set with her acting foibles, always late and often drunk. And then some women writers had rushed in to defend her and women in general. I had my own story to tell. I wanted to go to university later. Don't know if I considered myself brainy enough but I wanted to try. My parents supported that but my grandfather argued that it was a waste of time since, as a girl, I would only get married. He never made discouraging remarks about my brother. He was thinking of careers I suppose. I'm proud even today that my father took him to task for his words. And I went to university. But so few women of my generation went to university. It just wasn't expected. They mostly went into office jobs, banks or nursing.

Linda and I were no further forward with our strange young lad. Dennis backed off. I think he knew we were both annoyed but he had nothing useful to say. Linda and I didn't know what to do with ourselves. I felt uncomfortable and embarrassed as if, as girls, we had not known our place and were making a big fuss about nothing. I think Linda was more annoyed but equally feeling as if she didn't as if she didn't belong there at that moment. We somehow agreed to go home and Dennis joined the 'men' in their man shed.

In the evening, my Dad said he was walking to the library and did anyone want to go with him? He often took himself off like that and sometimes I went with him and sometimes I didn't. I don't remember anyone else ever going. I think he got books for Mum too. The library was further along from St Mary's church, on the corner, a low, modern building with not an awful lot of books to choose from. I suppose that I was at a difficult age … not quite an adult and not quite a child. Now I think there are books written for this age group. Young adults? Teen fiction? I was currently reading my way through Juliet Dymoke's historical novels and Linda sometimes leant me her books. We had both enjoyed Dodie Smith's 'I Capture the Castle'. But I said I'd go to the library with him and came back with a couple of novels and a book about ghosts.

The ghost book puzzled me then and puzzles me now. Why would I have picked that book when I was still professing not to believe in ghosts? I don't really believe in them now. Perhaps it was all part of my developing thinking, that I was beginning to question why I went to church, why I continued to be a Sunday School teacher and did God even exist in the first place? Add to that whether people had souls that went to Heaven when they died and if they didn't have souls, how could they possibly become ghosts? My mother dithered whenever I tried to discuss this with her. Later, when we'd moved away from Ribbleton, she loved her picturesque little Norman type church up on the hill in Penwortham and didn't want anything to disturb that. She liked it because it seemed to link her to the past and not because she was particularly religious. But my father said categorically that when you were dead, you were dead, and that was an end to it. No souls, no ghosts and dance on his grave if we wanted, although he did actually prefer cremation.

I decided to go up to bed early. Dad was watching a boxing match and Mum was doing whatever she did in the kitchen at night. I began reading. The short stories were exactly that, short, and I had already read two when Mum called up to say Linda was on the phone.

Without preliminaries, Linda said,

'We need to talk,' a line I felt had come straight from some television drama.

'What about?'

'Can't talk over the phone. We need to go some-where private tomorrow.'

I think I was amused by the cloak and dagger stuff, rather than intrigued.

'Well, what do you suggest? Do you want to come here?

'No, that's far too open. Parents and little brothers always about.'

I waited. I couldn't imagine what we had to share that was so secret, but that was Linda. She liked her confidential talks and would probably come up with something perfectly ordinary and common place in the end.

'Look, can we meet at the bus stop just up the road from my house tomorrow morning?

'Have we to pretend we're waiting for a bus? And talk in low voices?''

'No, we *will* be waiting for a bus. The one that goes to Gamull Lane.'

'Is that where we'll have our secret talks?'

I wasn't deliberately making fun of her. I couldn't help it. Gamull Lane was the terminus for the local service. It was as far as you could go in our area with the corporation bus service but it was an un-likely place for secret meetings. No deep, dark for-est for furtive transmissions. Linda didn't even no-tice my tone. She was deadly serious. She probably just thought I was entering into the spirit of the thing.

'There's a little park, almost as soon as you get off the bus. It's never busy. I thought we could sit on a bench there, away from everyone and have a picnic lunch. We'd look quite natural as we talk.'

'You mean just eat and talk?'

'Yes, what's wrong with that?'

'Nothing. It's a perfectly normal activity. Lots of people have packed lunches when they're working. And sit out on park benches to eat them'

117

'Yes, but it's the talking that's important for us. We're not just having a picnic but we'll look as if we are.'

'OK,' I said somewhat wearily. 'What time?'

'Late morning. So that we'll be eating at a normal eating time when we get there. We don't want to draw attention to ourselves. How long does it take to get to Gamull Lane from my stop?'

'Not long. And the buses are pretty frequent.'

'Right. About half eleven then. Is that OK?'

It was, and I went down stairs, hardly believing that all this conspiratorial scheming was an essential component of our rendez-vous.

There was nothing for a picnic either, only jam, and Mum said I would have to make the sandwiches myself. She was closing down for the day and not about to make a packed lunch without warning.

We had a walk in larder off the kitchen with shelves along both sides and a cold slab at the end. Most kitchens had one of those in lieu of a fridge.

I don't know when we got a fridge. There was an open tin of condensed milk on the slab. Oh, how I used to love that. Thick, sweet and totally sick making and delicious I would have loved to have taken that tin on our picnic but open, I could never have carried it safely. It would have dribbled out every-where, making everything sticky. I stuck my finger in the tin and had a slurp of the stuff anyway.

My ginger beer plant was on the slab too. I can't remember where I got my plant from and it wasn't even a plant at all. You had to set it up following a recipe and feed it ginger powder each day, leaving it in a cool place for ages. It would then start fermenting and sometimes, if you screwed the lid of the jam jar on too tightly, it would explode. Eventually, you could take off the ginger beer and create a new plant from the old one. I've forgotten most of the process.

I got rid of my plant in the end when I found I had more ginger beer than I knew what to do with. I don't think anyone bothers with them these days. I found a scrap end of cheese too and took that without asking, ready to suffer for the cause another time when Mum realised it was missing. So, it was with some decidedly boring jam sandwiches, a bit of dry cheese and an apple in my bag, that I went off to meet the wily Linda the next morning.

SIX

We didn't speak all the way through our short journey. In fact, we barely acknowledged one another at the bus stop, but then she hadn't asked for for a password!

Linda had glanced around as we got on the bus and no one got on with us. In fact, there was no one at all upstairs. Just a few housewives and an old man. Of course they could have been spies in disguise, but I thought not. I might have been grinning all over my face but Linda didn't notice. I followed Linda as she charged across the green at Gamull Lane and plonked herself on one of the many available benches. There were evidently no other spies competing for the secluded spots as she was able to choose which bench she wanted. She was biting into her first sandwich as she began to speak, still breathless from her offensive to take the bench.

'I think that Jack is a ghost.'

I didn't say a word. I was still unwrapping my jam sandwiches.

'It's the only possible explanation.'

I took a bite.

'I've thought about it a long time.'

It was strawberry jam and I preferred raspberry. I can't remember us having many more flavours in those days unless Mum had made lemon curd. Marmalade wasn't considered suitable for lunchtime sandwiches. Except that we called it dinner time where I'm from. It's that north v south divide again.

'There's nowhere else he could disappear to, is there? I think he goes back into the grave itself.'

Actually, I was beginning to lose my appetite, all this talk about graves and my remembrances of the boy Jack, his soaking clothes, his earthy odour, his deathly pale face. And why had I thought 'deathly'? I tried the cheese but it tasted peculiar after the sweetness of the jam. I gave up on it all and was wrapping everything up again just as Linda turned to me.

'What do you think?'

I let out a huge sigh as if I'd been thinking deeply all this time and said profoundly 'I don't know.'

We both sat in silence for some time. Linda was still eating. I looked with envy now at her potted meat. I supposed suggesting a swap was not appropriate at this juncture.

'I don't really believe in ghosts,' I finally said.

'She looked at me incredulously.

'But you have to.'

'Why?'

'Because you do. They're a fact of life.'

'Surely, if they're ghosts, they can't be a fact of *life*'?

I thought that was rather clever of me. Linda bristled.

'You know what I mean. Everyone believes in ghosts.'

'I don't think so. My Dad doesn't.'

'Well. You explain where this Jack comes from. I bet you can't.'

That much was true. I was not even beginning to

123

get that into my head.

'OK, so, where do *you* think Jack comes from then?' I asked.

'From the grave we've been tidying.'

'So, he must be one of the people named on the headstone? I don't remember a Jack.'

'We'll have to go and check.'

'And why has he suddenly started appearing?'

'He may not have just started. People haven't seen him before because there are never people around in that part of the cemetery.'

'And he flattened the plants we put in. When we chose that grave, it was completely overgrown and *not* flattened.'

'Oh, I don't know.' Linda was getting irritable. She wanted me convinced and I evidently wasn't. She seemed to have been chewing that bread a very long time. I reconsidered my own sandwiches.

'Maybe he had been resting in peace as the dead are supposed to do and we disturbed him?' This was Linda again. She took another bite.

It was a good supposition. I had to think for a while to counter it.

'But then surely every time one of the grave-diggers mowed around one of the graves, they would be disturbing other dead people?

Bodies would be popping up all over the place.'

The vision helped me make my decision. No sandwiches. But the vision, probably from some long forgotten scary film I'd seen as a terrified and impressionable child helped me to my next argument.

'And he doesn't wear a shroud. I thought all corpses were buried in a shroud.'

I had only a vague idea what a shroud might look like. In films they seemed to be long, floaty white things and Jack seemed to be in a normal shirt and trousers, though they looked old and worn. And soaked through too.

Linda obviously had no answer to that. She was still thinking though. And chewing. I wondered how she could, given our topic of conversation.

'Look,' she said finally, 'my book says ghosts come back from the dead because they have something left unfinished from the life they've left behind. Something they still want to do, they need to do.'

'What book?'

I thought of my own ghost book from the library, the two stories I'd read. A girl waiting for one of those old fashioned horse drawn carriages had seen a carriage draw up beside her, driven by a hideously deformed coachman. She had declined to get in because of the grotesque face. In the morning, she'd known it was a dream. But later that day, waiting for a real carriage, she'd declined to get in the one which arrived for her because the coachman resembled the gruesome driver of her dreams. That carriage had then been involved in a terrible disaster with all passengers killed or maimed. What had that told me about ghosts? Not a lot. Avoid travelling with ugly people?

The second story had been about two Edwardian

tourist ladies visiting King Louis X1V's Palace at Versailles. In the gardens they had met several people all dressed in the appropriate historical costumes, who had spoken to them and shown them all around the place and its gardens. The Edwardian ladies had not questioned their presence, had just assumed that the people were in some sort of historical pageant. They had asked interested questions and received seemingly accurate historical answers. Later, they had discovered that there had been no such spectacle taking place that day and it was thought that they had met up with ghosts. In fact, they later discovered that one of the ghosts supposedly bore a definite resemblance to Marie Antoinette, the ill-fated wife of Louis XV1.

The Edwardian ladies were actually named in my book but I couldn't remember either of them. In any case, that story told me nothing about ghosts either. Or about Jack? What had the book ghosts come back for? So, the coach driver wanted to save the young girl. But why her and not the other

127

passengers? And Marie Antoinette, what was she up to? And if Jack were a real ghost, what had he come back for?

'It's not really my book. It belongs to my father.'

I shook myself back to our conversation and started listening again.

'It's about exorcism, said Linda. 'That's what you call getting rid of ghosts.'

I must have looked puzzled. Why would a supposedly very serious and committed vicar have such a book? She could seemingly read my mind.

'Because when a soul is not at rest, it means a priest or vicar or someone has to come along to exorcise it. That means get rid of it, lay it to rest. There's a service the vicar has to follow to do all that. Actually I think there's more about it in Catholic churches. It mentions the Catholic Rites of Exorcism in my Dad's book.'

'You mean only Catholics become ghosts?'

'No, of course not, but they go on about the devil more. For them, it's more about casting out the devil than laying a soul to rest.'

'Has your father ever done one, an exorcism?

'I don't know, He wouldn't tell me, would he?'

'Couldn't you ask him?'

Linda looked aghast. Her eyes widened.

'Not unless I want to be kept at home for the rest of my life. I can't tell him we go wandering round the cemetery every day. He would want to know why I was asking. Cemeteries are holy and spiritual places for him. Not places for young girls to go gadding about in.'

'I'd hardly say we went gadding about.'

'Well, anyway, he probably wouldn't let me out again for a very long time. No thank you.'

'What else did you find out from this book then?'

'Oh, I can't remember. I can only read it when Dad's out and Mum's not noticing where I've got to. I'll try and have another go at it some time. It's in his office. What do you think we need to know next?'

Personally, I didn't want or need to know

anything next. Just talking about spooks was making me feel uncomfortable. And I didn't even believe in them. Sorry to keep repeating this but perhaps I was trying to convince myself. But Linda sounded as if she had a cause to pursue now. She was going to save this troubled soul and I knew, I just knew, that I was going to be expected to help her.

'I think we need to know the boy's name first,' she said. 'I can't really remember what it said on the headstone. We need to go and read it again and then if Jack reappears, check it out with him.'

I could tell that Linda was in sweeping all before her mode. She was on a mission. I was much more in favour of let's go and get some crisps. I'd noticed that there was a shop near the bus stop home and by this time, I was starving. I'd got the crisps and we were on the next bus before she could argue.

We went to the Youth Club that night but hadn't had a chance to talk about our ghost. I suppose, given all the previous secrecy, Linda wouldn't have allowed such talk anyway. She hadn't made me swear to secrecy, but I knew she would be outraged if I made a single move towards sharing our experiences with anyone else.

We'd played table tennis and even darts and some of the lads had come along during our table tennis session and coaxed us into that game where you have to form a circle and run round the table batting the next ping pong ball in turns as it came in. It was good fun but we suspected that it was only their sneaky way of getting their hands on the game itself, as we felt more or less obliged to slope off when it was finished and they took over the table. We walked home afterwards with Brenda and Eileen and so we met up at the cemetery the next afternoon with no plan in mind, bar reading the headstone again.

There was no sign of Jack or the grave-diggers and so we had all the time we needed. We'd talked as we walked through the modern section and neither of us could even remember the family name. It was the first thing we looked for when we arrived. The family name at the top of the tombstone was BANNISTER. It didn't mean a thing. There was a John, two Johns in fact, a baby named Alice, who didn't even make it to a month, and a woman whose name we now saw, after some hurried scraping away of lichen, was Sarah and who, we'd said, was Alice's mother. We had thought originally that the name might be Sandra, but there wasn't enough space for that, now we came to look properly and, in any case, when we considered, Sandra wasn't really a Victorian name. There was no Jack. I didn't want to sit near the grave in case our movement raised our ghost from his 'sleep' again and so we went and sat on a wooden bench near the water taps. I knew it was illogical. I still didn't believe in ghosts, but there you are. It may all have been my imagination but it was creepy.

'Well so much for our theories,' said Linda.

'We're no further forward. It was all guess work,

but I really thought we were on to something there.'

At first, I had been so relieved. No Jack, no ghost and just a lot of nonsense. And yet, I was the one mulling things over. I had an awful feeling that I didn't want to acknowledge. We were both silent for a while so that Linda didn't notice. I didn't want to put more ideas into her head but in the end I had to be truthful. You can't deceive a vicar's daughter!

'I may be wrong, but isn't Jack a nickname for John? Or a different form of the name or something? I think it's the same with Ian in Scotland.'

Linda's head rose again. Her face was creasing into a smile. It was as if she was wanting a ghost. I was the exact opposite.

'It's probably just a coincidence,' I said.

She was having none of that.

'Of course it's not. You're right. I've heard that too. I've always wondered why, because Jack is no shorter than John, but it helps us. John Bannister. Jack Bannister. He's the boy, John, on that head-stone. The fifteen year old son. That would be about right. And maybe he was called Jack so that people wouldn't confuse him with his father John.'

'Isn't he a bit small for a fifteen year old?'

'Weren't people smaller in those days?

'And if he died at that age, he must have been ill. Ill people usually don't have much of an appetite. Wouldn't that make him small and thin?'

I remembered going on a school trip to see the Bronte sisters' home in Haworth. I vaguely re-membered seeing samples of their shoes on display and thinking that they must have had such dainty feet. They were women but I also felt the memory of my teacher telling us that people are bigger and taller nowadays because they are so much healthier. We have better food, better medicines and we have bigger feet. We live longer too. I didn't tell Linda that. She didn't need any encouragement.

'I'm beginning to understand all this,' she

announced, 'Jack asked us where Dolly was. That's why he's restless. She's not in the grave with him and he wants her there. She was the member of the family he was most close to.'

'But maybe she was still alive when he died? Maybe she died somewhere else? Maybe the family moved away? There could be all sorts of reasons why she's not there. There must be lots of people who are buried away from their families. They surely don't all worry about each other and become ghosts?'

'Who knows?' mused Linda and looked wistfully around the immediate area as if there might be anxious family members all floating about in search of one another. I sat uneasily with that thought. But, an idea must have struck her as she suddenly jumped and raced back to our grave. Well not exactly to our grave; she ran from one nearby grave to another. She was scanning all the head stones and peering more closely at those which were difficult to read.

'No other Bannisters around here,' she declared. 'I'd thought Dolly might be nearby somewhere.'

'She might be somewhere else in the cemetery.'

'We could ask the diggers.'

But the diggers were nowhere to be seen that day and so we went for another ice cream. The next day, after a more devoted search, we found our gravediggers in a part of the cemetery we hadn't really bothered with before, which is probably why we had missed them the previous day. It was off to one side of the old cemetery with mostly modern graves which didn't really interest us. We obvious-ly hadn't looked any further than the ends of our noses because this section was mostly hidden by the overgrown bushes and trees which covered the rest of our old part. It turned out to be an area laid aside for people of non-Christian communities. We were able to identify a few Jewish graves by the stars of David on the stones and there seemed to be a growing number of Muslim symbols. I say 'growing' because those graves were modern and our friends were working on another intended to line up beside them.

I didn't know much about Muslims in those days though I'd had a Jewish boyfriend, who was actually just a friend of my cousins. He had told me he couldn't marry me because I wasn't Jewish and it would be forbidden. As we were both about 13 at the time, that hadn't worried me! Nor did we see each other much as he lived in Birkenhead, though we did write letters and once went to see some Norman Wisdom film at the cinema when my Mum left me with him on a visit to Liverpool to go and see some friends. My Mum was from Bootle, a place I'm actually quite proud of for some silly reason. I've always been a Ken Dodd fan too and we used to go and see him at Christmas at the Liverpool Empire. He still makes me laugh, something my husband doesn't understand at all! I even sought out his funeral to watch on You Tube. The documentary traced his life through his childhood and subsequent career as a comedian.

Anyway, all three of the diggers were hard at it and couldn't stop to talk. They said it was a 'rush job' which confused us. How could a burial be a 'rushed job' as the dead can surely wait?

I said exactly that. It was Arnold who told me why. 'Muslims have to be buried within twenty-four hours of their deaths. It's in their Koran, I think. The Koran, that's their holy book, and so this person, whoever he is, has to be in here tomorrow morning.'

'Could be a woman,' said Linda.

'It's a sensible thing really', said Dennis. 'Islam started in the hot countries of the world, in Saudi Arabia actually, and you couldn't leave a dead body around for long there. Too hot, flies, un-healthy. Know what I mean? '

'But this is England,' argued Joe. Even with hot weather here, it ain't that hot. And we have refrig-eration here too.'

'Yes, but you can't go looking at a thermometer every time you're about to bury someone. And they perhaps don't have thermometers in many parts of the world. The rural places, you know. And they wouldn't have had refrigeration when Islam began either would they? Or thermometers. It was about six hundred years ago. Fast burial was a sensible rule to have.'

'Well, they ought to abide by our rules here. This is not Saudi Arabia. These people are in England now.'

'But you can't go changing the rules just like that. The Koran is supposed to have been dictated out to the prophet Mohammed and he wrote what Allah told him to.'

Arnold glared at Dennis.

'You a Muslim then?'

'No, but I've learnt about it.'

'Well, why should we be working our butts off now for a rule that aint even Christian? Don't seem fair.'

'Well, never mind that now,' interrupted Linda.

She could probably see where things were going

and didn't want them to turn nasty. 'You said you hadn't time to talk but you're talking now. Perhaps you could carry on working and just answer a few questions for us? We need your help.'

'And we'd be ever so grateful,' I added, trying to soften their attitudes. 'Please.'

I said it in such a whiny, wheedling voice, that all three of them looked at me, glaring.

'What do you want to know?' Joe's voice was gruff and he struck at the earth with seeming venom. He obviously hadn't liked that young slip of a lad arguing with him.

'Well, we're looking for a grave with the name Dolly Bannister on it. Do you know if there is one anywhere here?'

'We can't be expected to remember the names of all the people in here. It's been a cemetery for hundreds of years.'

Dennis looked as if he was about to dispute that but Linda shut him up at once. She rushed in with another question.

Well, is there a register of all the names of the people here then?'

'A register?' the two older men looked at one another.

'A list,' said Dennis, helping out again. I could see how Dennis might be irritating. He inhabited a different world from Joe and Arnold. He was so much younger and seemed to know everything that they didn't. Or it seemed as if he did. They perhaps hadn't had the chance of his education. Or maybe he was just faster in his thought processes. What-ever it was, it didn't seem to go down well with them. And Dennis couldn't help it. After all, he was aiming to be a doctor. He was supposed to be clever. But maybe he had a few things to learn himself too in preparation for his future bedside manner?

'A list,' repeated Joe, 'You mean a record of who is buried here and where? '

'Exactly that,' said Linda. 'Is there one?'

'Well, why didn't you say so the first time?

141

There's one in the office.' He meant the old lock up shed at the other side of cemetery. 'Actually there's a few. They cover lots of years.'

'This has been a cemetery for hundreds of year,' Arnold repeated, as if intending to shut Dennis up again.

'May we look at it?' I asked. I added another please.

'Not now. We have a rush on, like we said.'

'Well how long will you be?'

'Not worth waiting. Depends on what the ground is like down below. Could be rocks and things to get through.'

'I tell you what we can do,' said Joe, softening, 'we can look at them when we close down tonight, before we go home, and tell you tomorrow.'

'What name was you looking for?'

'Dolly Bannister. Is she buried in here anywhere please?

'Dolly might be Dot, but most likely it would be Dorothy'.

'We would be most grateful.' This was Linda, and I was wondering if we were laying it on a bit thick now. But Joe and Arnold were nodding more happily and had forgotten Dennis and his know it all answers. Arnold even seemed to be mulling over what we'd said.

'Tell you something,' said Arnold, 'Bannister' is quite a common name around here. It's a Preston name. There'll be a lot of Bannisters in here I reck-on.'

'Well, we had a quick look around our-selves but there was only the one we know about already.

That's why we came to you.'

'And I'll tell you another thing,' Arnold contin-ued. 'That name Dolly Bannister rings a bell.'

'Not for me,' said Joe.

'Well ain't she supposed to be a ghost haunting around the market?

'The one that people said was killing young men years ago?'

'Aye, that's the one. It was afore my time, but mi Mam used to threaten me with her when I were a young un.'

Linda and I turned to look at one another. Our eyes must have widened.

'Aye, Mam said that Bannister Doll would get me if I got up to no good when I went out o' night. Not sure I knew what she meant then, but I did later. I never did get into trouble; never saw sight of her, I mean, or any ghost for that matter, but I was afeared at times. I didn't get up to no mischief.'

'It might not be her though,' said Joe, and we've never had ghosts here afore.'

Arnold was nodding in agreement.

'Not as we know of. Never had a murder here neither.'

I actually did not want it to be her. If the Dolly our ghost Jack was searching for was also a ghost and she was his sister, might she come looking for her brother? Two ghosts? We couldn't handle that. In fact, I really did not want to handle one. Can you even 'handle' a ghost? They can walk through doors can't they? But you know what I mean. Could ghosts communicate with one another? Could Jack have come to summon his sister?

'I tell you what,' said Joe, 'you go home for today. We'll have a look in our *register* and tell you what we find tomorrow.' And he smiled sweetly, whist also flashing a decidedly sarcastic grin, at Dennis.

SEVEN

Well obviously Linda and I were excited as we set off for the cemetery the next day, though I'm not sure if 'excited' was the appropriate word. Linda seemed excited. She was enjoying all this ghost malarkey whereas I was more apprehensive. And, as I kept repeating to myself, I was the one who didn't believe in ghosts. And if Linda did believe in them, she ought to have been more nervous than I was. We hadn't spoken much on the way home yesterday. We seemed to have both been struck dumb by those gravedigger revelations. If that boy Jack had someone in his family who was also a ghost, we were probably both too busy thinking of the consequences. Might we even be in danger? That was my reasoning. Linda seemed to be blithely barging ahead as if on a voyage of discovery. My thought was that if Dolly ghost had gone around killing people in the past, for reasons as yet unknown to us, shouldn't we be closing down our cemetery visits, not embarking on further dangerous investigations?

But all that was put aside for later as when we arrived at the cemetery gates, we weren't allowed in. There was a young looking policeman standing outside and the gates were firmly shut behind him. He stood in front of them trying to look important. He was unsmiling.

Since he didn't look old enough even to shave, we were not as impressed as we should perhaps have been, though he did have a thin little pencil moustache under his nose which looked as if it had taken months to grow and was supposed to give him a certain gravitas. But it made no impression on us.

'What are you doing here?' Linda began cheerfully.

The young lad looked disdainfully at her.

'I'm stopping anyone from going in.'

He probably thought that the answer was obvious and that we were stupid for asking.

'But why?' I said. 'Why can't we go in? What are we going to steal? It's a cemetery, not a jewellers.'

'Or a bank', I added for emphasis.

147

'I am not at liberty to say,' was the officer's superior reply.

'Well nobody else seems to want to go in,' Linda said, looking around widely. He shrugged. 'We won't do any harm. Come on, let us in.'

'I'm afraid I cannot do that. The cemetery is closed until further notice.'

'Come on,' I said, pulling at Linda's sleeve, 'we can go in at the other side. It's just a walk up Blackpool Road.'

'I wouldn't advise you to do that, 'said Constable Thin Moustache, 'I think you will find it closed at the other side too.'

'But why? You can tell us.'

'As I said, I am not at liberty to reveal that.'

He looked at us in a superior manner.

We both shrugged and gave him a corny, forced smile and wandered off somewhat aimlessly in the direction of Linda's house. Somewhere along the way we decided to keep on going and continued until we came to Blackpool Road. So, there would be another policeman at the other gates but we knew it was perfectly easy to get in without going through the gates. We remembered those iron railings which had been removed for the war effort and all we had to do was just step over the stone base and we would be in. We didn't even need to go very far but we continued past the shops on Blackpool Road so that we could hop over more discreetly, with only cars whizzing past and no eyes around.

We couldn't see a thing of interest when we stepped in and hid amongst the bushes along the cemetery edge. Everything looked as it usually did. However, we were looking out onto the modern section and realised that whatever was being hidden from public view might be higher up in the old part. All we had to do was step out onto Blackpool Road again and continue along until we reached the older area. It was even easier concealing ourselves there as the bushes were more overgrown, though we both collected a few scratched legs and I bloodied my socks. I was beginning to feel a bit nervous. I had a vision of a hand settling on my shoulder and saying something like 'you're nabbed.'

This time when we looked out, we could both hear voices. There was definitely something going on. We crept further in, breaking twigs and finding it uncomfortable and scratchy on our knees. We froze every time a twig broke. The noise seemed to reverberate so loudly around us that we expected to be discovered immediately.

Eventually, we felt near enough to what was happening to peer out again. It was easier to see now what was going on. All the voices and the commotion we now saw were on this side of the old cemetery, away from where our Bannister grave stood. Actually, we couldn't see anything much really but we were able to guess. We'd both seen enough television crime and police programmes where a sort of screen tent is put around a dead body. There was a tent out there and the commotion was all around it. We both instinctively crouched down and backed into the undergrowth so that we wouldn't catch anyone's attention and from there we watched intently as photographs were taken and men huddled around talking together. We couldn't make anything they said out. There were a couple of police cars parked up and some ordinary cars too. Really, it wasn't all that exciting after a while. We couldn't see a body and it had probably been taken away in any case. There was no ambulance in sight. We crept forward a bit again but still couldn't hear what they were saying. No sign of Dennis and his mates either. We were now sitting on the twigs we had snapped and soon had had enough of that too, with itchy and uncomfortable indentations on our derrieres and imagined creepies crawling up our legs, so we disappeared back into the main road where we sat on the rather lumpy wall. The lumps were the original stumps of the metal railings. We just looked at one another for a moment and then said almost simultaneously 'Dolly'.

'I hope not,' I exclaimed, having made my thoughts on two ghosts clear the day before. 'Can we go home now and give up this ghost business? Leave it to the professionals.'

'Of course not. It's just beginning to get interesting. And I can't do this on my own.'

'You have Dennis.'

Linda just tutted. 'Don't be silly. We are in this together. In any case, who are the professionals?'

I had no idea. Possibly the police? But I just gave her my vague look.

'Well, what are we going to do for the rest of the day?'

We had already started walking back down Blackpool Road and soon went past Linda's house on the main road and on to the shops beyond the cemetery. Our friendly police-man was still on duty and we waved as we passed him. He didn't wave back. He just turned and pretended to look the other way.

When we came to the ice cream shop, we broke with all tradition and went into the newsagent's next door. Whilst walking, we had decided that the best place to find out what had been going on in

Ribbleton Cemetery would be 'The Lancashire Evening Post.' But they didn't have today's edition. It was too early.

'We should go on to the library,' I suggested, 'that's where we could find things out.'

'They won't have today's paper either,' Linda said scornfully.

'No. I meant we could look up Dolly Bannister there. Don't libraries have past editions? If someone was going round killing young men in the past, surely that would be in the paper at the time?'

'What a brainbox!' exclaimed Linda. And she actually did seem impressed. We set off walking quite briskly. In our excitement, we even forgot to get an ice cream to help us on our way.

The librarian on duty was as young as our police man. Where were all the more experienced people when you needed them?

'We don't keep newspaper records here,' she exclaimed, 'You'll have to go to the central library in Preston. I think they have newspapers going back quite a long way, although the 'Lancashire Evening Post' wasn't always called that. It's had various names. I don't know what you should ask for but they will help you. What dates are you looking for?'

I looked at Linda. She looked at me. We had read the tombstone; we had sat alongside it numerous times. And yet we couldn't either of us come up with a date. Not a specific one anyway. The nineteenth century would hardly be good enough. Too vague. Nor did either of us have our library tickets in any case so that we couldn't even borrow a book to make all our traipsing around even moderately worthwhile. We had to abandon the visit. We were both despondent at first but then Linda perked up.

'Well at least we have a plan of campaign,' she said as we walked back.

'We do? A plan of campaign?'

'Yes. For tomorrow.

'For tomorrow?'

My face looked doubtful.

'Yes. For tomorrow. We go to the cemetery first

and hope we can get in. We ask Dennis and co what has been going on. Why has the place been closed all day? Then, we ask them if they checked their lists.'

'Registers', I corrected.

'Of course. If Dolly Banister is on one of their registers, we go and check out her grave. There should be a date on that.''

'And if she's not?'

'Well, we go back to our Bannister grave and try and work out rough dates from there. That's the best we can do.'

'And if Jack is there?'

'We try and get some more information out of him.

I must have looked doubtful again.

'Well, I've noticed he answers better if the questions are more specific. Like 'is Dolly your sister, aunt' and so on, rather than 'who is Dolly?'

'OK. So, 'how old is Dolly? Did she die? We can think of more tonight.'

'And then what?'

Well, I suppose we have to go into town to the central library and work from that.'

So, yes, I suppose we did have a plan of campaign.

There was no 'Lancashire Evening Post' in the porch when I got home. It was still too early. I sat and watched 'Crackerjack' with my brother and was restless all the way through, getting irritated by the childishness of the 'Double or Drop' game. Remembering now it was something to do with different kids, the competitors, having to keep hold of loads of different cumbersome prizes and some pretty enormous cabbages. You got a cabbage every time you got one of the quiz questions wrong. You had to struggle to hold everything and you were out with an annoying hooting noise if you let anything drop. The last one standing won everything within his or her grasp. When I watched it, the compere was someone called Eamonn Andrews. Meanwhile, the audience of other kids was making so much noise, shouting the competitors on, that I nearly missed the paper when it did eventually plop onto the porch tiles and Mum got there first.

'Oh,' I exclaimed and Mum looked at me, her eyebrows raised in surprise.

'I didn't know you were so interested in the news'.

'Well, no, I'm not normally. But I was wondering if there would be an item about Ribbleton there.'

She was scanning the front page and I was left to face the dreariness of the sports section at the back, as she held the paper upright in front of her.

'Is this what you mean?' and she turned the paper to me and read out … 'Body found in Preston Cemetery? A moment later, she read further down. 'It's the one in Ribbleton.

What do you know about that?'

For a moment she was frowning, looking at me archly, over her glasses like an irritable and very stern headmistress.

This was when I had to play the calm and casual person, instead of the agitated and eager one I really was.

'Nothing, really. It's just that there was a police

man on duty outside the cemetery gates today when we went past to go to Cuff's.' He wouldn't let any-one in. We wondered what was going on.'

'Oh,' she said, 'Cuff's eh? So, that's why you can never eat all your tea when you get home?' She was apparently more interested in my ice creams than in the fact that there was a dead body in the cemetery. She seemed not to have guessed that we had been frequenting the cemetery either. I'd said we had been walking past, which was true in a way.

She was probably not deliberately reading the ac-companying article as slowly as she could, but it felt like that to me. I wasn't even sure that I could have the paper even then but, without a word, she passed it to me and I slunk up to my room to read in peace. I tried not to rush. Slowly, slowly avoids Mum's suspicions. Mum went back to the kitchen. I couldn't believe that she had no   further questions.

I walked as calmly and as casually as I could up the stairs to my bedroom and then I read with the newspaper flat down on my bed and leaned over it, sitting on my feet. It was exciting that the existence of a body was confirmed. We'd worked that one out ourselves, when we'd seen the tent in the cemetery, but the article revealed nothing else, though our two gravediggers was involved.

MACABRE DISCOVERY AT CEMETERY

There was a call to the police this morning from the cemetery in Ribbleton, one of the largest in Preston.

Mr. Arnold Turner, one of the cemetery's two care-takers, made a grim discovery early this morning when he went to check that a grave prepared the day before was all ready for a ceremony later in the morning. He found the body of a young man with a serious head wound. He immediately contacted the Police who spent most of the day at the Cemetery carrying out preliminary investigations. The family of the victim has been informed, but he has as yet not been named. The victim was taken to Preston Royal Infirmary, but the head wound proved fatal.

159

Mr Turner, 57 years old, has worked for the Cemetery Authority for over 15 years, without similar incidents. His colleague, Mr Joe Atkinson, said the same. Both men were sent home for the day, after giving their statements and all burials scheduled for the day were cancelled. It is hoped that the burial programme can be resumed tomorrow.

There was no mention of Dennis. Perhaps he had a shorter working day than the other two and all the 'fun' was over by the time he arrived? And Arnold was only 57 years old. I'd have guessed older. That surprised me. I thought about ringing Linda but I knew her family took the 'Post' and that we wouldn't have been able to discuss the discovery without Mum, Dad and my brother all earwigging. She would be in the same position. And what was there to discuss? What had we learnt?

Well, nothing really. Except that the body was confirmed as dead. Linda and I had just assumed that. I tried to think slowly. I knew that as soon as I met up with Linda again, she would be running hard and jumping to all sorts of conclusions. I would be the one who would have to hold her back. How could we possibly know that the Dolly Arnold said he remembered from his childhood was the same as the one our Jack was calling for? How could we be sure that Arnold's memory was even correct? We had said Bannister and perhaps he had just latched on to that? I knew about the power of suggestion. There were so many ifs and buts and what ifs. Dolly Bannister terrorising Ribbleton Cemetery was about as likely as the Bogey Man living under the stairs who used to haunt some of the friends of my childhood. You rarely heard about him anymore. My parents had never invoked him. Even they said he didn't exist. And in any case, what was Dolly supposed to have done to misbehaving boys?

EIGHT

I didn't sleep very well that night. I practically ran up the road the next morning to meet Linda. We had agreed on a morning meet up so that we could go to town in the afternoon to do our library research. When I saw her coming the other way, we both ran.

'Did you see it last night?' she shouted as we came together.

'In the paper? Yes, I did. What do you think it means?'

We had both turned on our heels to make our way to the cemetery and could see from a distance that the gates were open. Well, I say 'both'. Linda swept me along. I was far from sure that I wanted to go anywhere near the place. A cemetery with a dead body in it. I realised how daft that sounded. Cemeteries are full of dead bodies but this was a presumably murdered dead body, found only the day before and was not the attraction to me that it appeared to be to her. However, I went along, a docile lamb to the slaughter, drawn forward by Linda's fearless enthusiasm.

'The first thing we do', she said, 'is see Dennis and the others.'

'They didn't mention Dennis in the paper though.'

'Yes, but he'll know as much as them. They'll have told him everything. They'll be full of it.'

There was no sign of them. We began to think that they had all perhaps gone to the Police Station to make their statements or that they were still being advised to remain at home. Was the cemetery still being considered a dangerous place? In which case, why were we there? I was quite ready to turn back but Linda decided to give it one last try and seek them out in their hut right at the other end of the cemetery.

And there they were, sitting as comfortably as lords with their mugs of tea and Arnold chewing on his pipe. Joe was reading about himself again in the newspaper he had brought to work with him, and Dennis, the innocent, was taking everything in so that he could reproduce it all again for his family

163

and friends that evening and in the future, whenever the opportunity might arise.

It was certainly Arnold and Joe's crowning moment. All three looked as if they'd been caught out skiving, when we walked in. We never thought to knock. They probably had been. Arnold removed his pipe and spoke for them all. He didn't wait for us ask him what had happened. He must have seen our anxious faces, eager to hear and yet not sure if hearing would agitate us further. He coughed, as if preparing to make a great speech.

'It were a big shock. It takes some recovering from,' the implication being that they needed time to do just that.

Hence the skiving.

'He weren't much older than young Dennis here', said Joe, 'Poor lad.'

'Did you all see him?' For a vicar's daughter, Linda was decidedly ghoulish.

'Aye, we did. As white as a sheet, he were.

Thought he were asleep at first.'

164

'He'd cracked his head on a tombstone,' Dennis explained. 'The question is, how did he get there? What was he doing there?'

'That's two questions.' That was Joe trying to make a point with Dennis.

'Did the Police work it out?' That was me trying to find out if the Police had thought anything was suspicious. I was wondering if the discovered body belonged to Jack.

'They didn't say nothing. Just sent us home and said as we should come back today.'

But Linda couldn't wait for all these
courtesies. 'Did you remember to check out Dolly Bannister in your registers?'

'No sign of her' declared Arnold. 'Another mystery.'

Dennis laughed 'You're on a wild goose chase.'

'Or rather a wild ghost chase', Dennis added. He laughed outrageously in spite of the solemnity of the occasion. He tried to straighten his face when he recollected himself, but he had been pleased with his joke and the smile kept creeping back.

I must admit I thought it was a pretty good quip too but knew we ought not to be laughing when a young boy had died here just a day ago. I thought we ought to leave, and Linda and I moved away in the direction of the Bannister grave. We had some working out to do. And we were so preoccupied with trying to put our thoughts together that we were quite taken aback when we arrived and saw Jack lying there in his usual pose. I even wondered if he had been waiting for us. The dead body couldn't have been Jack. The Police had taken that one away.

'Oh,' said Linda. She looked sort of pleased to see him. 'We haven't seen you for a day or two. We thought you'd gone.'

I found myself looking at the boy seriously. If he were a ghost I couldn't help wondering what he'd died from. He didn't have any wounds on him, no ancient bandages. It must have been some illness. I hoped he was no longer infectious. Could bacteria survive across so many years? I was only half

166

listening to the conversation Linda was trying to have with him.

'Did you find Dolly?'

He didn't answer. He didn't even look at her.

I had some ideas about illnesses from the past. My Mum was thought to have had Scarlet Fever and had been taken to what she called the Fever Hospital in Liverpool. Or could it have been Diphtheria? I had heard her talk about that too. Neither of them meant anything much to me. I think her sister, my Auntie Rita, had been admit-ted to the Fever Hospital too. Auntie Rita was my aunt in Llandudno. Their par-ents hadn't visited either of them there, which I think still rankled. Certainly my Mum spoke about it with a sense of injustice. I think I would have felt the same. But maybe they hadn't been allowed to for fear of passing the disease on to the other three sib-lings. Well, neither of the sisters had died and so perhaps Jack hadn't died of either of those, though even by my Mum's time, medicines must have improved since Jack had been alive.

Linda was still asking questions.

'Where is Dolly now?' And still getting no response.

What else was there? I'd heard about Dysentery. That always sounded nasty and I really didn't want to think about it. I could feel my nose puckering up as the idea passed through me. Sorry, that wasn't meant to be a joke! It was just the idea of diarrhoea spreading out distastefully everywhere. How did you deal with that in a world where you had to fetch water from a pump in the street, use old rags for cleaning and no one had a washing machine? And you could die from it; still could, in some parts of the world. I remembered the story of Haworth, where the famous Bronte sister writers lived. I recalled that their father had been a parson. Isn't that the same as a vicar like Linda's father? I was going off on a tangent again. Anyway, I remembered how the rain water, which filled the well beyond the Bronte's Parsonage, had come running down underground from the coffins in the churchyard before reaching the main source of water for the little town. All their drinking water must have been contaminated but they had never known. Yuk!

My stomach began to heave from all these putrid thoughts and lifted into the back of my throat, making me realise that I must at least have got over the nausea I had felt up to now every time I viewed poor Jack, with his pale skin, his damp and musty clothes, and the staleness of his whole being. It didn't seem to worry me so much now. He was even 'poor' Jack. Was I becoming hardened, or was I feeling sorry for him?

'Why do you want to find Dolly?'

I couldn't think of any more diseases except Tuberculosis. Was that the same as Consumption? All the Bronte sisters had died from that and then there was that character in some opera by Puccini. My parents had a record from it at home; 'La Boheme,' one of those large black 78 records. I may even still have it. I saved all their 78 records, though I never listen to them … 'Your tiny hand is frozen'. People got consumption because their homes were damp, cold, draughty and their food not very nourishing.

At least that's what I understood. But was that the case for the Brontes? Perhaps they got wet tramping across the moors?

But suddenly, Jack's voice stirred me awake. He didn't seem to be reacting to any of Linda's questions, just saying again what he wanted to say.

'Where is Dolly?'

His regular preoccupation. We were back where we'd started. Linda gave an irritated sigh and sat down on the stone edge of the grave. I remained standing. I may have been hardening but I still didn't want to get that near to him. She could have leaned out and touched him. Now, that, I reckoned, would have been interesting. Would her hand have passed through him like they were supposed to with ghosts? I wasn't about to try it. Linda seemed to recollect herself too and moved further back to sit on the grass. Perhaps it was her movement alongside him that stirred Jack? He seemed to move his head in her direction and look at her steadfastly.

'It's starting again,' he said and there was an anxious look on his face.

'All starting again.'

If Jack looked anxious, we must have looked puzzled.

'What's starting again?' I asked. I had crouched down beside Linda. I now considered her at a safe distance from the unpleasant body.

'The bodies. The bodies again. The bodies.'

Well, considering there were bodies all around us, dead ones, this seemed a bit non-sensical to us, until Linda shouted out in sudden inspiration.

'The murder yesterday. The boy who was killed here.'

We both stood up instantly and our eyes were aghast as they searched everywhere in sight. I'm not sure exactly what we were looking for but such an unpleasant feeling of dread had run through me and Linda's face showed her own horror. We were much too fast at putting ideas together. I knew she was thinking like me, remembering what Arnold had said; that he thought Dolly Banister had been killing young men around Preston Market years ago. She was the young woman who had been used like the Bogie Man to threaten youngsters into behaving themselves. Dolly Bannister would come and get them. OK, so we weren't young men but telling ourselves that didn't help. Were we looking for further dead young men like the one from the day before? We didn't see any, but the thought must have lodged in both our brains.

'Let's get the information we wanted from here and go,' I suggested. I just wanted to get out of there. All my old qualms had returned.

'What information?' flustered Linda. 'My brain has gone dead.'

'The dates.'

I fished out the pencil and paper I had brought with me and hesitated towards the tombstone. It must have disturbed Jack again.

'It's not true. It's not true.'

I looked down at him from above as I leant to copy the dates. Fortunately, he wasn't looking in my direction. I think I would have run away there and then if I had had to look directly into his face. He was still facing Linda. He couldn't seem to orientate towards sounds very well. He began again.

'It's not true. She didn't do it. She didn't.'

Linda just looked at me.

'Just get all the dates and then we can go. We can think about them later.'

It was hard to write resting on the stone-work. I could hardly read what I'd scribbled down. It was taking forever. I could feel my agitation carrying into the pencil. It was trembling as much as I was. Linda sounded to be getting agitated too. At least I was concentrating on the dates and trying to make them clear. As I scrumpled the paper into my pocket, she was already setting off. I ran after her. So, she wasn't as confident about ghosts as she claimed. And she had somehow manoeuvred me into climbing over Jack to write the dates. And where was she off to now? I blindly followed.

We stopped running when we reached the modern section. There were visitors replacing flowers and looking mournful. In contrast, we must have looked hair brained. A thought flashed through me, that we should maybe warn them about Jack or even about Dolly. But it would have sounded like nonsense. I wouldn't have believed it myself if someone had gabbled it all out like we probably would. And I didn't want to linger.

We stopped at the corner. We hadn't spoken all the way back. Now I felt myself panting. We had walked so fast.

'Shall we just drop the whole thing?' I suggested hopefully.

After all, nothing obliged us to investigate what was happening. It was the school holidays after all. There were plenty of other things we could do. I couldn't exactly think of anything at that moment, but there would be.

Linda nodded her head back and forth to show she

was thinking. I knew what was coming. She wouldn't be giving in. She was calm again now and her eyes were glowing with all the excitement of the chase. And I would be the compliant friend again, trotting dutifully and anxiously along behind.

'Let's sleep on it', I could hear her saying 'and then we can perhaps go into town tomorrow and do some of that research we discussed at the library.'

NINE

The Preston Harris Library, Museum and Art Gallery always intimidated me. It seemed such a prestigious building and in those days, I didn't even know what the word meant. It was like some ancient Greek palace illustrated in a history book. Wide steps rose up on each side of the building. You climbed them from ground level from the square and found yourself towering above the massive market square below. There were huge pillars reminiscent of that Greek palace again before you actually entered the building through wide, portentous doors. There was no need of any sign to remind visitors that this was a library and that you should remain quiet within the building. Whispering was the only possible form of communication in such a holy place. Who would have dared otherwise?

We had both visited before but were still awed by the vastness of the entrance area with its high reaching ceiling and hanging pendulum. I particularly remember that pendulum although I never

176

understood what it was there for. I remember there was a notice to tell everyone what they were seeing but even today I don't remember what it said. The thing swung to and fro on a regular stretch and probably moved around at a circular snail's pace as it did so. Was it something like Foucault's Pendulum? Was it actually Foucault's Pendulum? Certainly it was impressive whatever it was and our eyes attached themselves to it as it moved in its own hypnotic time. Is it still there in the library atrium?

When we both awoke from our mesmerised states, we looked around, wide eyed now, wondering where we ought to go to do our research. I remembered from a visit with my Dad that there was something he called a Reading Room somewhere to the right. I went in with him once while he enquired about something at the counter and I turned, a small child, almost attached to his leg for protection, to see lots of men in various attire supposedly reading newspapers, although some looked as if they might have been have been asleep, their heads lying still on the

177

paper in front of them. Their clothes suggested an air of poverty rather than the man about town informing himself of the day's events. Dad had said they were poor people in there to try and keep warm or sleep more comfortably than in a shop doorway. Frankly, I didn't want to go in there again, but as my Dad had evidently been making enquiries of some sort at the desk, perhaps that was where we should start.

How to begin? We both stood there timidly at the reception counter as a worthy, elderly lady looked wordlessly over her glasses at us from her desk and gave the slightest nod of her head to the much younger lady opposite her who seemed to be doing nothing more than shuffling papers around on her own desk. The nod must have signified 'you get up and deal with them.' She looked as if she had far better things to do than assist dithering teenagers. So, the younger lady got up and dealt with us. I be-gan.

'We've been trying to do some work for a social history project for school during the summer holidays.'

Linda turned to look at me. She seemed impressed. I don't know where all that came from. I must have instinctively realised that launching forth about the ghost in the cemetery might have been the end of her serious interest. Linda, good on her, was able to follow through.

'Yes,' she continued 'and we have been looking at the graves in the old cemetery in Ribbleton.'

My turn again. 'And we've been trying to find out as much as we can about one of the families buried there.'

'The Bannister family'.

The young woman looked rather helpless.

'You probably need the history section.'

'Or the Coroner's Office,' added the now interfering senior lady.'

Linda and I must have looked somewhat daunted.

'Where's that?'

'Oh, it's not here,' explained our younger assistant, eager to help with something she actually knew about.

'Or you could try the Archives. Do you have any dates?'

Delighted to have made progress at last, I produced my list from the tombstone. I had written it out again when I'd got home the evening before, as even I had had difficulty reading the lumps and bumps of the original.

'Mmmm … quite old. You might be better with the Archives.'

'Where would the Archives be?

'Or you could try the Registry Office.'

'Or you could see the Lancashire Evening Post people.'

I felt besieged. I had no idea where any of these places were; well perhaps the newspaper office, as we'd once gone to buy a photo from there after it had appeared in the paper. But the others, no; I must have looked bewildered. I turned to Linda. She shrugged. She was no wiser.

The elderly lady came to the desk. Perhaps she

wasn't so elderly. Thinking of Arnold at 57 had perhaps modified my opinion about what was old. Perhaps she was nicer than she'd first appeared too. She had taken her glasses off. She even looked quite kind. I mean I wore glasses for school work. And I was reasonably kind.

'Look I'll take your details and nip over to our reference section with you. After that you can stay on and do your own thing.'

We were profuse in our thanks. After all, we didn't need lots of details. We weren't writing a book. If we could just find out the basics, we could go home and forget about the whole nonsensical business. I didn't care if we never went to the cemetery again. All these tales of ghosts sprang from our underdeveloped brains. I was prepared to admit as much.

We followed our senior friend out of the reading room, through the main hall and landed up at another desk where she tutted into someone's ear
and then simply abandoned us.

'Right', said another librarian. I'll call her Miss In-between, as she was neither young nor old.

So, it was out with the social history thing again, for school, during the holidays and all that jazz, and I presented my names and dates list.

'Well, this sounds interesting. And so good you are working during your holidays. Well done!'

We basked in the praise, but really we just wanted her to find out what she could and move us forward. She must have read our minds.

'I'll just take these details to our historical reference filing cabinets and check them out for you. Let's see what comes up.'

She disappeared and we twiddled our thumbs for a while and stared around us. There were more people at desks, visitors this time, writing notes out of volumes of all kinds. Maybe that's what we would end up doing?

Miss Inbetween seemed to be away for a long time. She wasn't quite so perky and enthusiastic when she reappeared.

'You said you decided to study a family from one of the gravestones in the cemetery. What made you pick this family?'

Well, we'd felt, or perhaps it was only me who'd felt, that we'd been drawn to the place, but I didn't think I could say that. Meanwhile, Linda was rabbiting on about the range of ages on the stone, how they all seemed to be from one family and that the setting of the grave was attractive. Miss Inbetween was listening but she didn't seem happy about it. I couldn't think why it mattered. She considered for a while and then handed me my paper back.

'Well, I think you might be wise to work on another family. It's a lovely idea for a project, but I think it would be better for you if you moved to another headstone.'

There seemed to be something unsaid here. Linda and I looked at one another. We were both puzzled. How could she have sensed that our grave was a little strange? How could she possibly know that our grave was occupied by what Linda thought was a ghost? I still wasn't convinced about that myself but there was certainly something weird going on that I couldn't explain. Miss Inbetween even looked a bit nervous and flustered.

'What's the matter with our grave?' Linda had found her voice first. 'Why shouldn't we work on its headstone people?'

'Well, it's a bit hard to explain. I tell you what, I'll photocopy the reference I've found here to the Bannister family, and you can see why you should change your project. It might not be your Bannister family but nevertheless, I'm a bit concerned. Wait a moment.'

We were now agitated and flustered ourselves. We were excited too. It felt as if we were on the edge of some great discovery. We were remembering Arnold's words at the cemetery; that the name Dolly Bannister rang a bell. Why would a name we had never heard of until this month make Miss Inbetween so nervous?

When she handed us the photocopied papers, we

rushed through our thanks and hurried to the nearest empty table. Miss Inbetween called after us.

'By the way, there is a charge for photocopying but I'll waive it on this occasion, as it's your first time here'

It had never occurred to either of us that we might have had to pay for our information. As far as we were concerned, the library, any library, was a pub-lick service. We went to borrow books and had nev-er thought to be charged, not even when we received our original tickets. Perhaps Dad had paid for mine? He'd never said. We nodded our thanks and began to read.

The reading shocked us. Neither of us spoke. We just took it for granted that the Dolly Bannister men-tioned was our Dolly Bannister. We had nothing to say at first. I turned to Linda; she turned to me and we both began wordlessly to read again. Was it real? Was it true? Was it even possible?

We seemed to have stumbled upon something

beyond our experience. We had led such comfortable lives. We had no knowledge about the lives of others, except from our history and what we saw around us. What we were reading now was as another time, another place. They were real people but we were somehow estranged from them.

I think Linda took the print-outs home with her and I'm now remembering it in memory. This seems to me to be the essence of what we read. The articles didn't come from Dolly Bannister's time but from more modern writers.

So, what had we read that had so befuddled our senses? What had the librarian seen that had shocked her and made her concerned about the so called project we were working on?

This is what we read.

SPECTRE OF BEAUTY MURDERED BY HER OWN FATHER'S HANDS

The people of Preston, Lancashire, do not like to

mention the name of Dorothy, nicknamed the Bannister Doll. saying that just pronouncing her name is supposed to summon up her tormented spirit. They are quite rightly frightened of doing that. Dorothy was an attractive girl who lived in Preston in the nineteenth century. She lived with her father in an old tenement in Snow Street near the town's Walker Street.

Being attractive, the girl had many suitors so that the inevitable happened and Dolly, as she was better known, had to confess to her father that she was expecting a child. He did not react quite as well as he might, even though she knew he would be angry.

Her father gave her no sympathy at all. In fact, in an apoplectic rage, he dragged her out of the house, tied her to a stake in the garden and whipped her to death for bringing shame and embarrassment to her family.

Years later, a stone was erected to mark the spot where Dolly had been murdered. It was on the corner of Ladywell Street and Heatly Street. During *the years which followed, parent would bring their sons and daughters to the spot to show them the dire consequences of promiscuous behaviour.*

Dolly was buried in the grounds of Holy Trinity Church in Preston.

And then, mysteriously, the corpses of young men began to be found in Preston town centre. Their rib cages and skulls had been crushed to a pulp. The police had no success in apprehending the culprit. Rumours began to spread that Bannister Doll had risen from the grave to seek vengeance on these and all men for the way they had treated her and all women.

The murders eventually came to an end but sightings of Banister Doll did not. People claimed that at dusk they had seen the ghost of a young girl floating up Snow Hill. Just to see her had rendered them terrified. They all agreed that she oozed macabre feelings of evil.

When Dolly's father died, a new family moved into the house on Snow Street. They moved out again only two nights later saying that the evil Dolly had come to menace them. They never returned. Another family took over the house and only lasted three days.

Those claiming to see Bannister Doll seem to be frightened beyond fear. They say she exudes an aura of malevolence which chills them and which they are unable to shake off. And yet, in her lifetime, Dolly was a happy, outgoing girl, pretty and happy. Her death transformed her into an angry spirit.

What do you believe?

Is this just an urban ghost story?

When we had both finished reading, we got up without a word, tucked our chairs neatly under the table and walked out. Miss Inbetween was nowhere to be seen. We had no eyes for anyone else anyway. We lurched forward and out of the building. Back in the outside world, away from the numbing silence of the library, we seemed to come to our senses again. Perhaps it was the fresh air, the blue sky above? I felt better outside. But not a lot. We wanted to talk but thought that if anyone were to hear our discussion they would consider us warped. I certainly felt warped. I didn't even believe in ghosts for goodness sake. I was fed up of telling myself that. We sat on the bottom steps to the library, oblivious of the people going up them. We sat on the shady side, even though I soon felt cold and in need of the sun's warmth. At that moment, we were beyond noticing anything much. I've since read that the presence of a ghost makes you feel cold. I was ready then to believe that Dolly had followed us out of the library and was sitting on the steps alongside us. I was the first to speak, although it wasn't really language.

'Mmmm? ' I said, with query loud in my voice.

'Yes,' said Linda, knowing exactly what I meant.

'God almighty,' I said next, and then felt bad, realising that I might have shocked the vicar's daughter.

'It has to be said,' Linda agreed, shaking her head. 'What else is there to say?'

We had read that Dolly Bannister was indeed, was most probably, a ghost. That alone was possibly enough for us. After all it was in the paper. That, was evidence. The photocopied pieces we'd read had come from old newspapers. We hadn't yet come to the fake news of our future adult lives and largely accepted what we were told. What we had read was indisputably true. We had to believe it. Dolly ... she was acknowledged as Dorothy too ... had lived in Preston, though there were no dates in the article Miss Inbetween had photocopied for us. It vaguely said the early nineteenth century. There were no photographs of her either but there was a hand drawn picture of a young girl with long hair and glaring eyes. It said that this was how someone had seen her, with a face looking out of those eyes as blood streaked down the sides of her cheeks. We were wise enough to realise that this was just the fruit of someone's imagination for it said also that she has been an exceptionally pretty young girl in real life, so pretty in fact that young men had flocked

191

to court her. That had been her undoing. She had ended up getting pregnant and had to confess as much to her father. That's when all hell was let loose. That's when the Dolly Bannister Story, as it was called in the newspaper, started. Dolly was a ghost murderer.

Linda and I were both breathless, stopped dead in desperate disbelief for a moment.

'Do you believe it?' she asked me finally.

My brain was just coming round to thinking again.

'Why would anyone make such things up?

'Why did no-one stop her father from whipping her so much? There must have been people around?'

'Maybe he was too strong? Maybe he was the local bully? Maybe he was so incensed that nobody dared?'

Did we believe it? At that moment, we were just overawed that something we had thought was just a bit of nonsense in the cemetery was turning into something much more chilling.

But there was more. There were in fact two

photographs in another article. One showed Preston's Holy Trinity Church which was where Dolly was supposed to have been buried. The other was an old picture of Snow Hill where Dolly had lived. The caption said the row of terraced houses shown had now been demolished. The houses looked depressingly bleak but that was probably because all the windows had been smashed out and they all looked to be desolately empty. The photo must have been taken just before the demolition. There were steps going up to the front of each house, the number of them depending on where each house was on the slope of the hill. This was where ghost Dolly had been seen floating up Snow Hill and in the surrounding area.

'Why does it not say what happened to her father?

There's no mention of that. He surely can't have got away with killing his own daughter?'

'There's no mention of a trial either,' Linda agreed.

'I've never heard of Holy Trinity Church, I said.

'But your Dad will probably know where it is. And

where is Snow Hill?'

We would have to get a street plan of Preston.

Those people who claimed to have seen Dolly had spoken of the threatening menace in her face. And some advised that it was even dangerous to think or talk about her. The ghost could sense such talk and would bring her malevolence to those who dared to mention her name.

Again, Linda and I turned to face each other.

'Well that's us done for,' she said. I laughed nervously. So did she. But I could feel the hairs at the back of my neck rising with some kind of shivering chill. I was cold.

'And did you notice the bit that Arnold talked about that time?'

'Yes. That his Mum threatened him with Dolly; that Dolly would get him if he misbehaved. And look how it says parents would take their sons and daughters to the post where Dolly had been whipped so that they wouldn't behave in the same way themselves. I'm glad both boys and girls were warned.'

'Yes, but nobody whipped the boys, did they? It takes two to tango.'

'He didn't even ask her who it was, did he, her Dad? That's strange.'

'I expect there would have been quite a row. We don't know what was said. And then it was too late.

He couldn't ask her when she was dead, could he.'

'So, do you think this is what Jack meant when he said it was all starting again? That Dolly had started attacking young men again like the dead one in the cemetery?'

I had thought that too. But he couldn't have seen the dead man. He could scarcely sit up properly. Could ghosts perhaps 'sense' things like the article had suggested? Had Jack sensed the man lying there that night in the cemetery and thought it had been his sister who had killed him? If Dolly could 'sense' things too, perhaps she might turn her attention to us? We'd talked about her enough. And why did Jack not sense that his sister was there that night? And vice versa, if Dolly was looking for him?

I got off the step and pulled Linda up beside me. We sat in silence on the bus back to Ribbleton.

TEN

I searched the 'Lancashire Evening Post' that night. There was just a paragraph about the body in Ribbleton Cemetery. The Police were continuing with their enquiries and the family of the dead young man had been informed. That was it. No help to anybody, certainly not to Linda and me. So, the killing could have been the work of our Dolly. And I was beginning to think that if it was, I really didn't want to be in that cemetery, day or night. I'd been saying that from the start but Linda had never taken any notice. If Dolly's ghost could move around, she could move to find Linda and me. What if she could move to wherever we were? What if she could find us asleep in our beds? My imagination was not only running wild; it was in training for the next Olympic Games, probably for the hundred metres. Wasn't that the fastest race? I only slept because I lay awake for so long that I finally exhausted myself.

Linda rang the next morning and suggested another trip to Gamull Lane. I guessed that we were going to have a ghost council. That was infinitely better than going to the cemetery to pursue them in situ. After all, talking about Dolly was supposed to be danger-ous. Our conversation could draw her to us.

And there were two ghosts to consider now. Why did I never argue with Linda? Why couldn't I just say that I wanted to jack the whole thing in? And Mum said we had nothing for sandwiches again. It was jam and a banana. I was not bouncing with joy.

Our bench was vacant when we got off the bus. I started on my sandwiches before the talk could sully my appetite.

Linda opened with 'so, what are we going to do next?'

'I have no idea,' I said honestly. 'What is there to do? What can we do?'

'Oh, you can't give in that easily.'

'Well, I'd like to stay alive, please. I don't want my head caving in or my innards being turned inside out, thank you very much.'

'Oh, they won't hurt us. Ghosts can't do that.'

198

'Well other people seem to think they can. Why are people frightened of ghosts then?'

'Because they're from beyond the grave, beyond death. Nobody's been there and so everyone finds it a bit scary.'

'And it's not?'

'Not if you believe in God. He looks after those who believe in him.'

And that was probably my problem. I didn't really believe in God and I didn't believe in ghosts in the first place. No, I didn't understand it myself either!

'So, who killed those young men all those years ago? Everyone said it was the ghost of our Dolly.'

'Well, if it had been Dolly, the killings would have continued across the years. But they stopped, didn't they? And that's because it wasn't her.'

So, who was it then?'

'How the heck should I know? I wasn't alive then, was I? But it would have been a living person. Who stopped when he got caught for something else. Perhaps he was sent off to prison for a long time and

199

couldn't get out to murder? And he will have died long ago so that also explains why the murders aren't happening now.'

'And the young lad they found in the cemetery?'

'Just a coincidence. You'll see. And in any case, Dolly sounds as if she might have been quite a nice person. The lads all liked her. Jack still does. Not the sort to go around murdering people.'

'But that was before she had been wronged by someone.'

'That's not necessarily the case. She might have loved the person who got her pregnant. The papers always magnify the drama of things for their readers.'

'Right,' I said, 'and in the meantime?'

I gave her my most desperate look. That quietened her. We were back to her original question. What were we going to do next? I still had no idea and I waited until Linda was ready to explain our next move. She had evidently thought it all out the night before and obviously believed implicitly that I would follow where she led. The trouble was, I probably would.

'We have to go back to see Jack.'

I noticed that she now talked about him as if he were some sort of friend. He was Jack. You know, Jack at the cemetery. You know who I mean.

'And we have to check out if what he says matches up with the story from the library.'

'Oh, yes,' I argued, 'he's so chatty, he'll tell us everything we want to know.'

'Don't be like that. He will, if we ask him yes or no questions. I prepared some last night. I had the library photocopies to go through.'

I rolled my eyes heavenwards. I'd been glad yesterday that Linda had gone home with the papers, especially last night when I'd been thinking about ghosts 'sensing' things. If they could, I hoped Dolly would sense that it was Linda, not me, who had the writings about her. Totally selfish of me, I know, but there you are.

I listened now as Linda went through the questions

and I even added a few of my own. I think the picnic outing had just been to make me comply with whatever Linda had decided in the first place. If she had considered me shaky, she had been absolutely right. Now, I was backed into a corner and we were returning to that cemetery to interview a ghost, come what may. We waved to our grave digger friends as we passed. They all seemed to be digging out new graves in different parts of the modern section. Linda led the two of us firmly onwards. There was to be no loitering. Unfortunately, Jack hadn't been informed of Linda's plan and he failed to turn up. I shrugged and Linda looked disappointed.

'Ghosts obviously have minds of their own.' I said mischievously.

'Mmm,' she humphed peevishly.

'We could go back to see Dennis and the others,' I suggested, thinking that Dennis might prove an attraction for Linda, 'and ask if they have heard anything more about the dead lad they'd found here.' The Police might have kept them more informed than the general public. After all, they have to work around the crime scene.

We found Dennis on his own, a bit disgruntled because he'd been left to plank up the new graves whilst his colleagues went for a cup of tea in their shed. There had been no further details about the incident. They hadn't even seen the Police. We told him about our visit to the library and about the chilling tale of Dolly Bannister. He looked satisfyingly shocked.

'Oh Lord!' he exclaimed, and then went quiet. He climbed up out of the grave and said he would go and tell the 'boys'. We personally thought he'd suddenly found he was scared of being on his own in a haunted cemetery, and down a grave too, and had gone for some moral support. A sweet tea perhaps? Isn't that what they give people in shock? We couldn't blame him.

We chuckled our way back at Dennis's expense to 'our' grave and were then shocked ourselves to find Jack lying there in his usual damp and lifeless pose.

It suddenly struck me that perhaps Jack had been given morphine on his way to dying and that that was why he was always in such a dozy state. Wasn't morphine called opium in Jack's time? And it almost immediately also struck me that Dolly would not have had any morphine and would, therefore, be a lively and active ghost in comparison to her brother. Then, I had another thought. Would opium have stayed in the body over all these years? I had no idea, but if Dolly hadn't had it, she would be able to move about and search for her so-called enemies. This seemed quite logical to me at the time, but perhaps not very scientific. I didn't want to think about that and instead watched Linda as she collected herself together and waved a hand to attract Jack's attention as she brought out her prepared questions from her pocket.

'Hello, Jack,' she said cosily, as if we'd known him for years. 'We meet again. I'm so glad as we wanted to ask you some questions about yourself. You're such an interesting person, you know.'

This was quite weird. Here we were, chatting amiably in an ancient graveyard to a boy who had been dead for who knew how many years,

Jack's head seemed to turn slightly in our direction. If there was a flicker of interest, it was hardly noticeable. But Linda went on.

'You've mentioned Dolly to us. Is she your sister?'

We sensed the shadow of a smile on Jack's face.

Linda smiled too. 'Ah,' she said, 'and was Dolly kind to you when your Mum died. Did she look after you?'

There was that shadow again and perhaps even the slightest nod.

'How did you know ...? I began.

Linda turned towards me, her face excitedly flushed.

Just guessed. 'Look at the headstone.'

And Sarah, I guessed alongside her, whose name began the family list on the stone, was the mother. I heard Linda ask that very question and receive the barest nod in reply.

Linda was positively beaming.

'So, the man here with you, the one called John, was your father?'

A look of horror passed over Jack's face. It was the clearest visual movement we had seen. Linda and I both knew what the father had done. Did that explain the horror? I was thinking that this might be the end of our ghostly chat, that we had made a dreadful assumption that might send Jack reeling back to wherever he came from. But he just lay there and then we heard a very distinct word come sharply towards us.

'Grandad.'

We suddenly had a vivid picture of the whole family before us. The mother, Sarah, and her baby daughter, little Alice. There was a brother who had died before our Jack and lastly there was Grandad John. The vision silenced us. We both stood stock still thinking about them all, the life they had led together, happy until …? There was no mention of Dolly and there was no 'father of the above', presumably husband to Sarah. It was as if we were mourning all those who lay there together. We wondered what had happened to the father. Had he been carted off to prison? We certainly hoped so.

And it was then, as we stood side by side, in quiet respect, that we heard a twig crack behind us. Our silence magnified the noise. We could hear the grass moving from alongside the graves beyond ours as footsteps progressed towards us. All that grass that we had so carefully cleared had grown again over the summer weeks. It was long and dry and rustling, ready to shed its seeds. I had never noticed the awful and resounding noise it made before. The sound of cautious footsteps was whispering into my ears and trickling a chill into them which spread to the back of my neck. I felt the icy tingle of it seizing me there and then spreading all over my body.

We neither of us moved, both frozen to the spot, ours ears trained on the steady approach of the foot-steps. Each step seemed thunderous to us now as they grew nearer. We held ourselves still and in absolute silence. Neither of us dared to turn in their direction. I felt rather than saw Linda clutch at her throat. It was as if both of us had turned to stone where we stood although I could hear and feel my heart beating so loudly. Then I saw Linda move in what seemed like slow motion, trying to extract something from around her neck beneath her blouse, trying to get to it with scarcely a move. I saw that it was her confirmation crucifix. I'd been given one too, but I never wore it. I understood straight away. She was going to use the crucifix to save herself. Remnants of old Dracula films flashed before my eyes. She would stretch it out towards the phantom and dismiss it with some sort of oath from God. I understood every movement she made, what she was doing, how she was thinking. But there was nothing to save me. I wasn't wearing my confirmation crucifix. I didn't even know where it was. Was this Dolly Bannister come to get us? I couldn't turn round. I couldn't look into the menacing eyes people had described in the newspaper. I didn't want to see the blood trickling down the sides of those perilous, glaring spaces. I braced myself to feel Dolly's hand dig into my chest and tear forth my heart. Anxious shivers raced up and down my spine. I stiffened, ready to feel the piercing pain. And Linda moved the crucifix upwards and held it before her as she slowly began to turn round to face whatever was coming. I remember wondering if she was the last thing I would see before I died, before I saw the menacing eyes of the ghost of Dolly Bannister staring ominously across at me.

I heard Linda gasp. 'Oh God'.

Was she beginning a prayer? As a true and spirited vicar's daughter? It was what I expected. She was still holding the crucifix before her. And when I saw her body crumple. I imagined the worst … Dolly's hand reaching out to her. I prepared to run, but felt fixed to the ground.

'Oh God,' she said, 'you didn't half frighten us.'

Her body crumpling had been her relaxing. I turned and saw why. I felt mine doing the same thing. And likewise, I also invoked the name of the Almighty. There was Dennis standing before us. He was smiling. He had probably just realised how he had scared the living daylights out of us. He laughed as Linda and I just hugged one another. We didn't really want to give Dennis the satisfaction of knowing that he had just freaked us out. Especially since he had always thought our ghost tales were so funny and that we had imagined everything. But we really couldn't help it. Relief surged through us.

But slowly we became aware of Dennis in his turn becoming suddenly very still. We turned and understood. We stopped our nervous laughing to look at him. His body had solidified where he was, just as ours had. He was standing like a stone, as if his shoes held him to fixed to the ground. He was looking down upon the pale and limp body of Jack lying in the grave space.

'So, it's true,' he said in a whisper. 'We laughed at you. Joe and Arnold said you were two silly girls. They thought you were trying to wind them up. Or just being giddy girls with over vivid imaginations '

'Don't be afraid,' said Linda. She was smiling now. I'd thought she might be annoyed at the 'two silly girls' comment but I was smiling too. We'd had the last laugh so to speak. Dennis had become almost as white faced as Jack himself. I thought he looked as if might be sick. I sniggered as I thought to myself ... he looks as if he's seen a ghost!

'This is Jack,' I said light heartedly, waving a hand vaguely in our ghost's direction, trying to brighten the situation a little, pretending it was as normal as introducing someone at a party, as if we had total control of the proceedings. 'I'd like to say that he's our friendly neighbourhood ghost but he's not all that friendly. And he's not all that chatty either. But how would you feel if you'd died from tuberculosis?'

'Is that what he died from?' Dennis asked cautiously taking a step away from the graveside.

'Well, we don't actually know, but you have to do a lot of guessing around here.'

We should ask him,' Linda was bright with enthu-siasm, 'Why did we never think of that before? It's an easy yes or no answer.'

But it wasn't. Jack just looked at us. Linda and I were disappointed. We had wanted to show off our ghost, present, correct and even speaking.

'Perhaps he doesn't know the word 'tuberculosis'?' I said and tried again with 'consumption'.

Still no reaction.

'Perhaps he doesn't even realise he's dead.' Den-nis was pondering out loud. 'Some people slip away so quietly between life and death that sometimes no one notices that they've gone. Or perhaps he doesn't know what killed him.'

'Who died first, you or Dolly?' I suddenly asked, turning abruptly to Jack.

There was a definite answer then. He said 'Dolly' quite clearly and there might have been something that resembled a tear, though Jack's eyes were pretty watery most of the time and it was difficult to tell.

'Maybe when he died, he was expecting to be

buried with his sister and when he discovered that she wasn't there with him, the disappointment was what brought him to the surface again. He's looking for her.' Dennis seemed to have relaxed. He was joining us in trying to sort things out in our heads.

'Yes that's what we thought,' I said, 'but he must be pretty patient, don't you think, as he's been missing her for a very long time now? I'd have given up by now.'

'Ah, but he's got all eternity, 'Linda laughed,

'And nothing else to do.'

'Which is more than I have?' Dennis was looking at his watch. 'I've missed my tea break too. I'll tell Joe and Arnold that I've seen your ghost. See what they say.'

Linda and I had got so used to having Jack between us that we just said goodbye without a second's thought and sauntered off to Cuffs for our ice creams. I didn't even think about looking in the paper for further news about the cemetery body until Dad slung the newspaper down as he switched on

213

the television.

And then I sat up. There it was. The report on the murder. It seemed that several young men had come forward to report what had happened. There had been a group of them. They had been mooching about, wondering what to do with themselves and come up with the idea of buying bottles of cider at a local off licence. They had gone into the cemetery to drink them, hidden amongst the bushes of the old section. Quite a good idea, actually, I thought, as the cemetery at night was not a place I would have chosen for a late evening walk, even without a possible attack from Dolly Banister. There would have been few people around to see them and report them. And they didn't know about Jack and Dolly. In a group, they would have been quite confident of their safety. They had got in as we had that time by climbing over the iron railing stumps. They were all under eighteen apparently. The messing about had continued and under the influence of the alcohol had got rowdier and rowdier, which was stupid of them.

They were calling attention to themselves when they had hidden themselves in the cemetery to avoid detection on the first place. Still, I don't suppose young lads in a drunken stupor, as they must have been by that time, were in any position to think things through logically. Nor would members of the public be likely to want to challenge them. Then, there had been some scuffles and one of them had fallen against a tombstone and knocked himself out. That's what they had said anyway. It had most definitely been an accident but the lad had died.

When the incident found its way into the newspapers, they all initially clammed up in fear, until that same newspaper, a day later, mentioned the licenced victualler as having reported a number of boys buying cider and then recognised the photo of the victim. The lads must have realised that there was no escape and rather than wait for the police to descend on them, they went en masse to declare themselves. End of story. What would happen to them was not disclosed.

For us, it didn't matter anyway. It had not been Dolly. We were relieved in some strange way. As if we had formed an attachment to the family and wanted to be on their side. Dolly had had a hard time. She was the one who had been murdered. The whole family, apart from that horrible father, had suffered.

So that was that. There had not been a murder a such and Dolly was in no way responsible.

It was both a relief and a disappointment. It was a relief to know that there was no reason now to fear the menacing face of the ghost and her arms reaching out and tightening into your chest. The disappointment was that, with safety now assured, I could tell myself that our ghost hunt was not as exciting as it might have been. As if I'd been enjoying it!

We were visiting my grandmother in Liverpool the next day and so I wouldn't be meeting up with Linda. It's a funny thing about my grandmother. I hadn't realised that she was my grandmother until quite late on. She had apparently wanted to be called

Auntie Nan and I never thought beyond that. I didn't have a paternal grandmother. She had most definitely died and I just thought this Auntie Nan was one of the many others aunties my brother and I had. When the truth did finally dawn, I never understood the auntie bit. Perhaps it was her way of feeling younger than she actually was. She certainly never behaved much like a grandmother. Or much like an auntie either, for that matter. I don't remember ever having a birthday or Christmas present from her.

Anyway, I thought I'd ring Linda to see if she had read the good news. She had, and when I reminded her that I wouldn't be there the next day, she said that she would be following up the Church of the Holy Trinity information we had and could manage on her own. According to our papers from the library, Dolly had been buried in the graveyard of the Holy Trinity Church in Preston and we neither of us knew where it was. She was going to the cemetery to see if Joe and Arnold knew.

Arnold and Joe knew alright, said Linda the next day. When I looked pleased, she told me not to bother. Joe and Arnold had once spent a long time transferring coffins between Holy Trinity and other churches because Holy Trinity was due for demolition. It had eventually been destroyed sometime in the 1950s and presumably built over long ago. Joe thought there was now a car park where it had been.

So, it was all a dead end, so to speak. Just as we had been thinking about going and searching in another church graveyard, the plan had been scuttled.

'Where did they take all the coffins? Can they remember?'

'They said to lots of different churches. Not all churches have a graveyard apparently. Ours doesn't, does it? They took them to wherever was nearby, or if there were still relatives around, where the relatives requested them to be taken.'

'So, Dolly could be anywhere. Where was the church originally?'

'Joe thought it was in a square called Trinity

Square and then he said that was somewhere near Friargate, the old Snow Hill area. It was quite rural in those days. And Snow Hill, if you remember, was given in that article as where Dolly used to live. It all fits together. '

'So, there's nothing more we can do.' I couldn't believe I was disappointed after all the fear and worry I had previously felt. It seemed stupid.

'Well ... 'Linda looked at me, her face distorted into what looked like a mischievous smile.

'Well, maybe.'

I waited. She was obviously ringing something out for all it was worth.

'Dennis wondered if his uncle might be able to help.'

I was puzzled. Linda explained.

'Do you remember when we first met Dennis, we thought it was a strange job for a student to do as a holiday job? And he said that his uncle had got it for him because his uncle is something to do with whoever organises the cemeteries in Preston?'

I remembered. 'And …?'

'Well, he thought his uncle might be able to find out where Dolly is now. He waffled on quite a lot; said records have been kept for births, deaths and marriages for years. He thought they even went back to Henry V111's time, though official rules had come in and countless adjustments had been made over time. He thought that when Joe and Arnold moved the coffins from Holy Trinity, there would have had to be records made about where they all went. It was quite interesting listening to him. Even Joe and Arnold said so.'

'So, we could perhaps find out where Dolly is after all?'

'If Dennis will ask his uncle.'

'Did he say he would?'

'He said he'd try.'

'So, we just have to wait.'

Dennis's uncle seemed to take a long time. There were only about two weeks before school started again and we wouldn't have time to visit the cemetery once homework started up again. Linda had a longer school day than I did. She had to get a bus into town every morning and then take another bus to Lytham, a much longer ride than mine into town and out to Moor Park. Sometimes, I even went on my bike. Linda then had to repeat the process in reverse after school to come home. It would soon start getting dark too early for us to meet up then. I certainly didn't want to be venturing forth into the cemetery in the gathering gloom. Maybe Jack wasn't the only soul who wasn't resting in peace.

Linda and I were lost during the wait. We popped into the cemetery each morning when we could, to see if there was anything happening. No news. We drifted off aimlessly wondering what to do with ourselves. We caught a bus into town to go shopping. No money. We soon lost interest in that. We revisited the Harris Museum and drifted around in there. No talking. We walked to Brookfield Park. In those days, you could pass through a wooden passage way at the bottom of Stuart Road and cross the railways lines which ran from Preston to Longridge. There was even a sort of decaying platform there when Ribbleton must have been an important stopping place. The trains ran very infrequently now but the drivers always waved if someone was there to see them. The short cut was blocked off in my last year at Greenlands, which annoyed so many people who then had to walk the long way round down Cromwell Road to get to their home on the Brookfield Estate.

Brookfield Park was scarcely the kind of park we know today. Is it even there these days? Probably covered over with more houses now. There were no amusements, no cute little café. It was more like a large piece of spare land left behind after all the council house building, but there was a rather dirty looking brook along the bottom edge which I had played at jumping over many times with my friends from Greenlands County Primary School. I once lost my shoes in there when I had taken them off to paddle and someone's younger brother had thrown them both in. And my socks with them. The current, faster than we'd realised, had carried them off, probably to Courtaulds factory some miles away, beyond Gamull Lane. My brother will probably remind me of the time I dropped him in the waters trying to jump the stream with him in my arms. The ice cream van was calling and we'd been given some money to buy one each. I knew there wasn't time to walk the long way round with him and I was an expert stream jumper. Just not that day! And not with him in my arms! He cried all the way back home, much to my embarrassment.

There were regular onlookers as we jumped the brook, who told us that the water was contaminated, full of chemicals from the factory works. We would die; was that true? Which way did the stream flow? We had no idea and we didn't care. The future was too far away from us then. Linda and I even met some of the former school friends I'd had at Greenlands, as many of them lived on the Brookfield estate. We recognised each other but both sides studiously ignored the people we had been best friends with then. That had been another life and was gone now. We had all moved on to different schools. The 11 plus exam of those days had sadly separated us for ever. My school, the Park School for Girls, a grammar school, held a meeting for parents when the plan to move to comprehensive schools was first muted in Preston. My Dad's hand was the only one raised to vote for comprehensive education that evening. Even my Mum voted against him. Well, she would wouldn't she, as long as I went to the grammar school? I was with my Dad on that one.

The day did eventually dawn when Dennis told us that his uncle had done his research. And yes, when Holy Trinity Church had been destroyed, the coffins had been relocated according to the wishes of those relatives who were still around to acknowledge their owners. Not many people had bothered apparently, but those who did, all agreed that the remains should be sited together in the graveyard of All Saints Church in the centre of Preston. It was felt that this would make the remains accessible to the greatest number of people.

There was, however, a grisly tale to tell and I think Dennis enjoyed the telling. His uncle really had no memory of what had happened. He was far too young at the time to have participated or even observed. But he had managed to locate an elderly former colleague who knew a man who also knew a man who actually did. Most of the coffins had rotted along with most of the bodies. There were just some bones, some teeth and some clumps of straggly hair. Sometimes these macabre remnants could be linked to a plaque on the outside of the coffin, saying who they were and when they died. More often though, they couldn't, so that all of those anonymous souls were put together as having once been buried in the former Holy Trinity Church. The rest were coffined separately and reburied as required. With one exception. Strangely enough, the man who knew a man and so on, could precisely

225

remember the fate of Dolly Bannister.

Poor Dolly. She had become famous in her time, but it was a fame which had not served her well. Her death at the hands of her father became very well-known and her connection with the dead young men was particularly remembered. Those people who did claim their long dead nearest and dearest did not want their relatives' bones mixing with those of Dolly. Unbelievably, there was prejudice even amongst the dead. They claimed there would be some kind of spiritual contamination if Dolly came into contact in any way with their self-righteous and long gone relations.

'So, what happened to her then in the end?' I asked.

'Well, Dolly's coffin was found relatively intact so that they knew it was her inside. There was apparently a bigger plaque on her cover explaining who she was and what she was guilty of, so that anyone coming into contact with her remains in future years would know to be wary and proceed with caution.'

'But she wasn't guilty of anything.' I was appalled at the dreadful treatment meted out to this fun loving, pretty girl.

'She was promiscuous by the standards of her time,' explained Dennis.

'No better than she should be,' Linda added. 'I've often wondered what that phrase meant. That's what they used to say about young girls who got themselves into trouble.'

'They never said it about the boys though, did they? They were just 'sowing their wild oats'. Isn't that their phrase? All good fun if you were a boy.

What a two faced lot they were in those days. I supposed they still were to some extent. For every girl who transgressed, there must have been at least one boy. But that was OK. I wondered again what did happen to that father who whipped his daughter so hard that she died?'

Dennis shrugged. 'I've no idea.'

'Would your Uncle's informer know?'

'Don't know that either. I could ask.'

'Please would you. And so where did Dolly's remains end up?'

'They were put in a separate coffin and buried away from all the other graves, in a corner of the graveyard.'

'Was it in consecrated ground?' I asked. 'I've heard that criminals were often buried outside the churchyard because it was felt that they had behaved in an ungodly way.'

'I think it must have been consecrated. The corners would all be part of the Church's property.'

'Oh, well that's good,' Linda joined in,' and actually it might help us, as the grave will be easier to identify if it's in a corner. And it can be got at without disturbing anyone else.'

Dennis must have been able to see what was coming next. How could he possibly have guessed what Linda was thinking? Perhaps they were closer than I'd realised.

'God, you can't just go round digging graves up',

he said. 'You two are the limit.'

'Not me,' I argued, 'I wasn't thinking of doing that. That's the last thing I would want to do.' I could feel my face crunching up in disgust. It was true. I could understand Linda wanting to find the grave but I really hadn't expected her to want to dig it up. I wasn't going to say a word.

'Well I want to,' admitted Linda 'Not personally, but we do know some grave diggers.'

'You can't do it just like that. You have to get a special licence or something. It's got to be official.'

'Well they excavate graves on TV.' Linda was not giving up. 'When they want to find out if someone's been murdered with poison or whatever.'

'Yes, but that would be official. With a licence. There's got to be some point to it all. What are you digging Dolly up for? It's exhuming a body by the by the way, not excavating.'

'OK. But you knew what I meant.'

'So, why are *we* wanting to exhume her?'

'To put her with the rest of her family, of course.'

S.DAVEY

Linda beamed at us all. Wasn't it obvious?

She explained when Dennis and I scowled at her.

'Jack is a ghost because he has unfinished business to sort out in the real world. That's why ghosts come back. I've read about it. He's missing his sister in the grave with him. So, he materialises to try and find her. She must have been special for him when he was little. Do you remember, he agreed that she'd looked after him when their Mother died? He wouldn't want to be parted from the rest of the family, his Mum, his Grandad and so the obvious solution is to bring Dolly to him. We need to move Dolly's coffin to the same grave as Jack's. Once re united, he will be happy. Everyone will be happy and they can all then rest in eternal peace. We won't see Jack the ghost ever again.'

'Amen,' said Dennis. Now, can I get this straight?

So, what you're planning is that Dolly is removed from the All Saints' Cemetery. She is to be brought to Ribbleton Cemetery and reinterred here?

Linda nodded.

Dennis' eyebrows lifted and he continued.

'Who have you got in mind to do all the digging? The digging at All Saints and the digging up of the Bannister grave here to make room for Dolly?'

'Will there be enough room in the Bannister grave for one more?' I asked. 'How many coffins can you have in one grave?'

'I have no idea.' Dennis shook his head as if it was all madness. 'Joe and Arnold will probably know, but in any case, it's immaterial. You can't possibly think that we can do this. On our own. Don't forget, Dolly will have to be transported somehow from All Saints to here. How do you propose to get over that little problem? Not to mention all the others I've mentioned?'

Linda looked at him coolly. As if these were minor issues. It was as if she had the smug satisfaction of knowing that God would provide, her being the vicar's daughter and all.

'I never once said we had to do it all on our own. I even said we knew some gravediggers. Joe and

Arnold. Three actually if we include you, unless you're going to walk out on us, now that things are becoming more complicated.'

Dennis began to remonstrate. 'That's not fair. Of course I'll help.'

Linda smiled. I had the funny feeling that she had in some subtle way bound Dennis to her by questioning his integrity. I'm not sure that he liked being bossed about though. She seemed to have long ago forgotten that she was trying to charm him. In fact, the two of us had become so embroiled in this saga that we had forgotten about lots of things. Like the next Youth Club Dance on Saturday. Were we even going? Like Frank Ridden and Dave Appleton. We never talked about them now. We still went to the Youth Club on Wednesday and Sunday nights but, well, things were somehow different.

'Right', Linda went on. 'So that's the digging sorted. We have three strong and experienced grave-diggers. Now, didn't you once say that Joe and Arnold have a van for cemetery use?'

Dennis nodded. 'For carrying planking, tools and stuff.'

'Right, well that's the transporting organised as well. A van to carry Dolly's coffin. All that's left to do is get official permission to do everything and get Joe and Arnold on our side.'

'Won't we have to pay for some of these things? Or are we just hoping everyone will help us out of the goodness of their hearts?' I knew I had no money to spare. I certainly didn't want to spend what little I had on satisfying a ghost.

'Well, we haven't got any money and so they'll just have to. I never said it would be easy.'

'You can't do much these days without having to pay for it. And there'll be rules and regulations. Are you proposing that we break the law? Do all this at night when no-one's looking?'

'No, I'm hoping that you, Dennis, will talk to your uncle again and find out what it all entails.'

'He'll want to know why I'm asking.'

'Well, tell him. I think we have come to the point

when we have to come clean and tell others what is going on. We'll just tell those people who need to know. We don't want the press queuing up to watch and join in.'

'Who then?'

'Well, us three obviously, Joe and Arnold to dig and drive, your uncle and anyone your uncle says we need to see, and my Dad.'

'Your Dad?' Dennis and I were horrified in unison. Perhaps for different reasons?

'Yes, my Dad. I'll have to talk to him about it all. You can't just dig up graves without thinking of the people buried in them. Even ordinary people would need prayers, but these are ghosts. We have to settle them back down again to be sure they don't start haunting again.'

'Are you talking about exorcism?' Dennis asked.

I was beginning to feel brain dead. This was all beyond me. At least Dennis seemed to be understanding what she was talking about.

Linda was totally in control.

'Yes. It won't be easy, but I'll have to ask to see him about something important and then talk him into it. I'll probably get into trouble but I have to do it. It's my duty.'

'Your Dad?' Dennis didn't understand this last bit.

'Yes, he's a vicar. He can do the exorcism.'

You could almost see the penny drop as it filtered onto Dennis's face.

It must have cost Linda to reveal that. She usually didn't tell people about her Dad if they didn't know her and I had learned not to mention it either. She didn't like people knowing. People began treating her with deference and she hated that. She was not a deferent sort of person. Strange that! Teenage rebellion on her part perhaps? But here she was deferring in all the ways her religion expected. None of it would have occurred to me. I hadn't been taught deference of any kind. Deference wasn't the same as politeness. I had certainly been taught that. My Dad said religion didn't matter 'a toot.' Was I going to have to tell him too? He didn't believe in ghosts either, I reminded myself again. 'Dead is dead', he always said, 'and that's that'.

Dennis had obviously been thinking.

'What kind of vicar?'

'What do you mean?' I asked, not understanding.

'Catholic or Anglican or what?'

'Does it matter?' I asked again.

'Anglican. And it matters to my Dad.' That was Linda making the position totally clear.

Now that I understood, and wondered what would happen if Dolly had been a Catholic? Would it make her worse if Anglican prayers were said over her coffin? It ought not to have done as far as I was concerned, but people are funny about religion sometimes. Well a lot of the time, really. And they were particularly bothered about such things in history. That I did know.

'Dolly must have been Anglican.' Linda said, with what sounded like pride. She must have known what I was thinking. 'Because they buried her in the Anglican part of the graveyard.'

'Yes,' Dennis agreed. 'And these things were important in those days.'

'They are important now,' said Linda emphatically. She was definitely proving to be her father's daughter. More than I had ever realised. She looked steadfastly at Dennis. Her eyes seemed to hold him in her gaze. I sensed the tension between them. I breathed deeply and kept my silence whilst I thought.

Were these things important to Dennis, the student at Preston Catholic College? Would this be where he opted out? And his uncle? On religious grounds? And I was wondering whether Linda would have done all this if Dolly had been Catholic. Her father's contribution would certainly have been in doubt. I remembered again that she wasn't even allowed to go to the local Methodist Church when we had special church parades for the Guides.

I realised the significance of that now. I had never thought about it much before. It's funny how you learn about people. I suppose this is what they mean by a growing up moment. I looked at Linda and then

237

I looked at Dennis. What was I going to learn about him?

'OK,' said Dennis. 'So I'm going to ask my uncle to find out what we need to do next and get back to you. I suppose you want me to talk to Joe and Arnold as well?'

The slight moment of tension passed. I smiled at Dennis. I was pleased with him.

No-one had worried about what I thought.

In the end, I thought that perhaps I ought to tell my Dad. I wouldn't want him hearing about it all from someone at the local shops or on a visit to the library. I didn't know how other people were going to hear about our exploits to be able to tell him, but you never knew. Mum too, I supposed, though she would just be aghast at the idea of our having been meddling in cemeteries for the whole of the summer holidays. Dad would just say it was all a lot of poppycock but he would be interested and might even join us at the exorcism as a matter of curiosity, regarding how daft other people could sometimes be. He would like to see his views upheld.

Mum would be different. I remembered her once telling me some tale about an event after her first husband had died. Her friend's husband had been the captain of some ship that went down during the second world war. All hands lost. This friend, actually she was called Dorothy had persuaded Mum to go to a séance with her so that they could call up their respective husbands. They were told that they had to take along something special which had belonged to their husbands for the 'caller'… what do you call the person in charge of a séance? … to use to summon the presence of the loved one. I remember … a medium. Not many people had cars in those days. Mum certainly did not and in the end she never learnt to drive and so on this occasion she put some personal, sentimental items in a box and fixed the box with string onto the back of her second hand bike. The box with all its sentimental pieces had disappeared by the time she arrived at the séance hall. So much for Mum's knots! Perhaps it had fallen off the back as she peddled her way along but even after retracing her route, the box never reappeared. She missed the séance, lost all the things she had held important and never did get in touch with her dear first husband. Forever after, she believed it had been a message from him telling her not to dabble in the supernatural. It had been a lesson for her and she had never forgotten it. She would not come to the cemetery. It was a misguided thing to do. The vicar's presence would make no difference. Worse, she would not want me to go. I was banking on my Dad's curiosity carrying the day.

My predictions about my parents turned out to be satisfyingly accurate. They both reacted just as I'd foretold. I hadn't been as sure about Linda's father. I thought he might forbid her spending any more time in the cemetery for the rest of the holidays. Perhaps I would be eliminated from the vicarage too, as a bad influence. In the event, when Linda reported back, it turned out that he was perfectly willing to carry out an exorcism, though he said that he would have to inform the Bishop of the Diocese. He'd also said he had to be sure that neither Linda nor I were suffering from any kind of mental illness.

Apparently, disturbed people are regularly encountering things like ghosts. It was good to know he didn't think we belonged to such a category. He'd actually heard of the Dolly Bannister story and explained that though she might be considered 'possessed by evil spirits; which had made her kill with so much cruelty, our ghost Jack probably wasn't. The exorcism would be for her. Jack would just need our prayers to help him rest in peace.

That all made sense, though my Dad used his usual rich vocabulary to dispute that any one was ever evil or possessed by evil spirits. It was all in the way they had been brought up. Or it was a bona fida mental illness.

I had also imagined that Dennis's uncle would dismiss him the second time his nephew came calling for help. But he didn't. He even produced a reference about where we would find Dolly's 'new' grave in the All Saints' churchyard.

The only people who demurred about helping were Joe and Arnold. It wasn't about not being paid when we first mentioned it. They initially imagined that we were going to do it surreptitiously at night and I reckon that spooked them a bit. The menace of Dolly seemed more real to them than all the rest of us. But when they heard that we had a vicar involved, they were reassured. It seemed they felt the hand of God would be protecting them. I felt more relieved that my Dad would be there. My brother asked if he could come and was mortified to be denied.

The only thing which bothered Joe and Arnold was the fact that they hadn't ever seen Jack. They were not convinced that it was not all some silly nonsense on the two 'silly girls' parts'. They were even a bit annoyed that Dennis had now seen Jack when it was their graveyard and surely they should have been the people to see him above all others? Dennis brought them along to the Bannister grave one afternoon when Linda and I were both there. There was no

Jack that day.

'Well, we've never seen him rise up from the ground,' I said. He's always been there when we arrive.'

'We've never seen him sink back down again either,' agreed Linda.

'The ground doesn't even look disturbed,' said Joe. And that was true. All the weeding and digging we had done way back at the beginning of summer was no longer in evidence. Everything had dried over. The White Rock and Sedum plants were still there. They might even have been said to be flourishing even though we had never watered them since those early days. The Love in a Mist had dried up but there were big fat pods at the end of the stems threatening to explode any time soon.

We had downed tools when Jack appeared. Neither of us wanted to touch the ground that had brought him forth. We had never discussed stopping our 'gardening'. It was just what felt to be the right thing to do. And we didn't want to encourage the emergence of any other family members.

Dennis told us that, now that Joe and Arnold knew where the grave was, they had nipped over on their own a few times when the cemetery was on the point of closing and there were few people around. They seemed to think that popping up unexpectedly on the plot would give them a better chance of surprising Jack. They were irritated that he was never there.

I was worried. 'What if they change their minds about helping? If they never see Jack they might decide that it's all a big con after all. Why should they believe us?'

Come to think of it, we hadn't seen Jack much lately either. What if he had found peace on his own and we were all wasting our time? He might have settled into acceptance.

Dennis and the two gravediggers went off to their work and Linda and I settled on the grass again for what was left of the afternoon. Linda shuffled on the grass and leaned forward as if to speak to the

244

people in the unseen coffins.

'I think we should tell him,' she said quietly.

'Tell him what? And who are you talking about?' I settled alongside her.

'Jack. Tell him what we have been arranging for him and Dolly. It ought to please him. It's a family reunion. Tell him about Joe and Arnold and what their part in the plan is. And tell him that if Joe and Arnold never get to see him they might change their minds about helping. Tell him he has to appear to Joe and Arnold. That might make him come.'

'Do you think he can hear us from inside there? That he can think about what he's doing?'

Linda shrugged. 'Who knows? It's all we've got. Why should we be the only people he appears for?

'Dennis saw him.'

'Yes, but he was there when we arrived and then Dennis came over later. Perhaps he can't disappear when people are around and he had to wait until we had all gone.'

My turn to shrug, but we both leaned over and began

talking in turn to the grave soil. Anybody passing by would have wondered what on earth we were doing, would have thought that we were a pair of weirdos, but isn't that what people do all the time in cemeteries … talk to their dear departed, telling

them what's been going on, how much they miss them, asking for advice even?

We told Jack everything we knew about him and what we had planned for him and his sister. We said he needed to appear to the two gravediggers who worked in the cemetery so that they would keep to their role in helping him. We said he had to appear or else! Not that we knew what the 'else' could be for someone who was already dead. We just wanted him to get the message. Then we went home.

ELEVEN

Now it was just a matter of waiting, waiting until everything was ready for us to proceed. We didn't go to the cemetery very often now. Everything seemed to be coming to a natural end. Well the school holidays certainly were. But almost the last time we visited, we saw two jubilant gravediggers. They had at last come across Jack on one of their surprise pops-ins.

'We was amazed, 'said Joe. 'It were after work at the end of the day and we just decided to pass by there.'

'Aye,' agreed Arnold. 'We nearly didn't go. It was just coming on to rain.'

'And there he was, just lying there. I nearly jumped out of my skin.'

'We'd got used to there being nobody.'

'Did you speak to him?' I asked.

'No thank you very much. But he was there just like you said he looked.

'All wet, pale and as dozy as a dead donkey.'

Linda and I were delighted. Both diggers were on board now for doing the exorcism. They didn't want Jack or any other ghost around when they were working in the cemetery over the darker months of autumn and winter. It grew dark very early in those months and the gloom was an unsettling experience in any graveyard, however used they were to it. We told him that Jack was a harmless ghost but they weren't having it. A ghost is a ghost and who knows what he could transform into? And there was Dolly to think about too. She was the one with the terrible reputation. No, they didn't want to meet her. They were convinced now.

In the meantime, Linda and I went into town to see Dolly's grave. We found it quite easily. It was on its own at the edge of the graveyard looking lonely, for-lorn and completely overgrown. We overcame the desire to tidy it up a bit. We remembered what that had led to the last time. A ghostly Dolly was the last thing we wanted to see. We sat alongside her and told her what our plans were for her and her

248

brother. We told her we were trying to help her and that she should not think there was something amiss and try to escape. We told her all about her brother looking for her. She should stay where she was and she would eventually be reunited with her family in their grave.

Linda and I looked at one another. Even we thought we were daft. Linda said a prayer and waved her crucifix over the mound. I felt as if keeping my fingers crossed might be just as useful too.

TWELVE

It was a lovely late summer's evening when we all gathered at the cemetery gates for the special exorcism ceremony for Jack and Dolly. Linda, Dennis and I had been back at school for a few weeks already. Linda and I hadn't met up during those weeks for anything to do with Jack and his sister. We'd both started working hard towards our 'O' levels and Dennis too had started in the sixth form. We hadn't seen him either. At least I hadn't. Perhaps he and Linda had met up? I had too much homework and thought the others must have been the same, although Linda and I had gone to the Youth Club on Wednesdays and Sunday evenings. And we'd walked home as usual with Eileen and Brenda on those occasions and not mentioned the last time we'd been with our ghostly 'friend.' We all went to the first Youth Club dance of the new term but although Dennis had brought a friend, nothing happened between any of us. In any case, Linda didn't seem all that interested in Dennis now. She had

returned to her adoration of Dave Appleton and I
certainly didn't like Dennis's somewhat geeky
friend, Nigel. Apparently, according to Dennis, he
was the cleverest boy in the school. He was certainly
not for either of us. I think Linda and Dennis had
kept in touch though because I'd heard Dennis ask
for her telephone number before we went back to
school. I wondered if they were going out together
now but I didn't ask and she never said anything. I
didn't think I minded but maybe I would have liked
to have known if there was something between
them. It didn't look as if there was, but how would I
know? They each kept to themselves, as if they were
embarrassed. I felt annoyed about that, about the
mystery, I mean. It made me feel even more out in
the cold. That was perhaps because she'd also made
another friend on her school bus to Lytham. She was
a new girl, from Longridge, and she even started
coming over to the Youth Club sometimes. I felt
truly out of it, their gossip about people I didn't
know, their shared laughter and so on. Mum said

that two was company and three was a crowd.

Linda had set the exorcism meeting up and as we gathered, there was a strange atmosphere between us all. There was just Dad and I from our house. Mum was at home with my brother but she had given me a wreath to lay on the earth after the ceremony. Actually, I think she'd made it herself as she'd been doing a flower arranging course at Evening Classes and I recognised some of the flowers from our garden amongst the ivy and the holly. I didn't think we could have afforded a posh, shop-bought wreath, but this one looked pretty good.

Dad and I were the first to arrive. We had agreed to meet up at the cemetery gates. It was about half an hour before closing time and the evening was beginning to draw in. I stood there feeling somewhat uncomfortable with the wreath in my hands at this time of day. But then Dennis arrived, on his own, and I introduced him to Dad. I said he was one of the gravediggers but Dennis was quick to say that it had only been a holiday job. I think I'd embarrassed him and when the real gravediggers arrived, I was glad they hadn't heard. They already thought Dennis was a bit too big for his boots. I thought it was good that he'd done the job, dirty and a bit creepy as it was. I guessed that there would be few students who had done grave digging for a holiday job. All the gravediggers looked clean and smart, no longer the dirty old, or young, men we should avoid.

Linda and her father arrived last and there were introductions all round. We all became very serious after that as we walked up the avenue of the modern section and onwards to the old part. There were no other people around and it would have been scary if we hadn't been a sizeable band. We placed ourselves around the grave. I'd been worried that Jack might have turned up for the occasion and been lying in wait for us when we arrived. That would have been a surprise for everyone.

But the surprise was all mine. Joe and Arnold had been busy. The grave had been dug out and covered all around by a green sort of material. I think it was meant to look like grass. I'd spent so much time in the cemetery but I'd not seen a grave all ready to be used before. Not having been to a funeral before, I had no idea what to expect. Though I suppose this wasn't actually a funeral in any case. I leaned forward but could see nothing below. I'd been expecting to see at least Grandad Bannister's coffin on top but everything had been hidden. And there, on one side, was Dolly's coffin, waiting to be lowered. She had a plain and simple coffin but it looked clean and new. How had that happened? Had someone forked out for a new coffin for her? Maybe from church funds or perhaps Dennis's uncle had organised it? I though it better not to mention it. I didn't want to have to pay.

Linda's father was just putting a sort of sash around his neck and finding his place in his book of prayers when we heard footsteps. We all turned in unison and saw an unknown man approaching. He looked a bit flashy to me. I could see he had been smoking. He stubbed his cigarette out on Jack's neighbour's gravestone. I think we must all have frowned at him when he did that.

'Sorry,' he began. 'Didn't mean to startle anyone. I'm from the 'Lancashire Evening Post' He held out an identifying card. My Dad looked at it and nodded, but questioningly.

'Mind if I stay?'

I think we all felt that it was Linda's Dad who was in charge and it was he who replied very formally.

'As long as you respect what we are doing. This is a serious business and you should not take photographs during the ceremony. You should certainly not smoke.'

The man repeated his apologies and settled himself in our circle in a suitably serious manner.

'How did you know about this?' I wouldn't have dared say a word but the vicar was Linda's father and I suppose he didn't worry her.

'Someone from the Cemeteries Department rang the office and wondered if an exorcism might be of interest us. I wasn't busy and so thought I'd pop along to see what's what. I've never seen one before. Can someone tell me what is going on?'

'Perhaps afterwards,' said Linda's Dad. 'For now we require respect and silence.'

And we all bowed out heads. I listened but didn't remember very much afterwards. There was some-thing about protecting people from the devil and asking for help to drive out evil from our own hearts. At one point, the vicar moved towards Dolly's coffin and held up his hand as he said prayers over her. He asked for peace for all who slept here in God's gar-den and we all said the Lord's Prayer. Then Arnold and Joe lowered Dolly into the grave and there were more prayers and requests for God's help again. Linda produced some sprigs of flowers ... was the good old White Rock still flowering? ... and we threw those onto the coffin. Then we all picked up some earth and threw that down too. Finally, we said the Lord's Prayer again and at last, we were able to depart in peace, as the Vicar said. I gave my wreath to Joe who said he'd put it on the mound when he and Arnold had finished refilling the grave. I found myself giving them both a kiss on the cheek as I thanked them. They were both remarkably clean, which helped! We left them both there. My father shook their hands.

As we walked back I heard Linda telling the newspaper man all about Dolly and Jack. She didn't tell him about Jack as a ghost, otherwise, if people came to see where they ghosts had been, Jack might never be sleeping in peace. Nor Dolly and the other family members. People would come to see where they all were. There would be nothing to see but that wouldn't stop them. She just told a story about reuniting a family in which a great wrong had taken place. It sounded like we had done an exceedingly good thing. I was impressed. I heard my name mentioned and Dennis's too. And then the newspaper man asked if he could take a photo of us all. My Dad said yes, though I think the vicar would have replied otherwise. My Dad pre-empted him. The reporter took one of us, all just as we came out of the old cemetery and then Linda continued to talk to him, and my father and Linda's walked back together through the new section.

That left Dennis and me bringing up the rear.

'I suppose this is the end,' he said. 'The end of the summer and the end of Jack and Dolly. I hope they're happy together. Not like me and my sister. We're forever squabbling.'

I looked at him with interest. I had never really spoken to him properly before. We didn't even know his second name or where he lived. Or that he had a sister. I'd left the personal talk to Linda. She had claimed him when we'd first met him. I asked him now.

'Dennis Seddon,' he said, 'and I live down Cromwell Road. Just over the railway bridge.'

'Lambert Road?'

He nodded.

Goodness. 'We're practically neighbours.'

'Yes, I've sometimes seen you on the bus going into town in the morning for school. I get on at the stop before yours.'

I had never noticed him. Just shows you what a school uniform can do. I always kept my head down when wearing it and avoided eye contact. But I looked at him now. I didn't always get that bus and, if I did, it was usually so packed I had to go downstairs. I usually found myself refused. I was always annoyed if I had to walk on up to the main road. Now I could see that he was actually quite good looking. He had dressed himself up for the occasion and looked quite smart. He was smiling.

'I was wondering,' he began, 'now that we are all back at school and it will start getting dark earlier, if you would like to meet up again sometime.'

'You mean all of us, Linda as well?'

'No, just you and me.'

I was silent for a while. They say all is fair in love and war, but shouldn't I be respecting Linda here? But she hadn't seemed to be as interested in Dennis lately. She had been so pre-occupied by the exorcism and then when we met up at the Youth Club again, she was with her new school friend who had always stayed for tea. I had never been invited to stay to tea. I didn't need to be as I lived just down the road and this new friend lived in Longridge, which was quite a distance away. Still. I felt I had been cast aside in a way. I looked at Dennis again. He had thick dark hair with just a bit of curl. Just what I like. How come I had never noticed his lovely brown eyes before?   And he was asking me out after seeing me in my uniform and my clod hopper shoes! And the school hat we had to wear! That was flatter-ing!

'I thought you liked Linda, not me?

'Now why should you think that?'

It's just that you seemed to talk to her more. You didn't notice me.'

'She talked to me. You are the quiet one.'

'So, are you asking me out?'

'I suppose I am. Yes, I am. So what do you say?'

But we'd reached the gates at the cemetery

entrance. We all said our goodbyes. I said I'd see Linda at the Youth Club on Sunday. She went off with her father. I explained to my Dad that Dennis lived on Lambert Road. The fastest way to Lambert Road was down Stuart Road and then along where I lived and turn right at the end. So, that's the way we went, Dennis, Dad and me. Dad chattered on about where Dennis went to school and I can't remember what else. How was I going to give Dennis his answer with Dad chaperoning me all the way home? When we got to our house, Dad said cheerio to Dennis and went in. That was clever of him. I lingered for a moment. Dennis looked at me.

'Well?'

'Yes.'

'Seven thirty then. Inside the Arcade. Saturday. Is that OK?'

I nodded and then he smiled and walked off. I knew exactly where the Arcade was… the Miller Arcade, a collection of rather posh shops in the shape of a cross, with a kiosk at the intersection point. In the town centre. It was where the young couples in Preston met up for dates. I'd never met up with anyone at the Arcade for a date before but I knew that I would be there this time. Saturday, seven thirty.

ACKNOWLEDGEMENTS

In remembering my youth, I also remember my parents who gave me a very happy childhood and always did their best for me.

My brother gets a mention in my novel and he supported my idea of writing this. We discussed Bannister Doll. She was a well- known Preston ghost at one time. You can Google her!

Thanks too to my daughter for being my first reader and to my husband for being the second. I have followed their advice and edited accordingly.

I must also thank my loyal friends, Chris and Dianna Haggerty and Marie Mervill. I hope they will long continue to support me and buy my books!

I was Sylvia McKillop when I lived in Preston until my marriage. Hello to anyone who recognises me via this name.

I can be contacted by email:

sylves@hotmail.co.uk.

I have also written three novels about the Cathars, a religious group, who lived in the Pyrenees in southern France in the thirteenth century. They were persecuted by the French Inquisition. All my main characters are authentic, taken from their depositions in the Inquisitional registers.

'PRIEST': the story of Pierre Clergue, the rapacious priest of the remote village of Montaillou in the Pyrenees.

'JUMPING FROM THE TOWER': the life of the last Cathar holy man, Guillaume Belibaste, and the man, Arnaud Sicre, who hunted him down.

BEATRICE: the story of Beatrice de Planisolles, her life as Chatelaine of Montaillou and her struggles to be an independent woman in a world made for men.

All available from Amazon.

S.DAVEY

Printed in Great Britain
by Amazon

18735397R10154